NECESSARY VOICES

A COLLECTION OF SHORT FICTION

MERLE MOLOFSKY

NECESSARY VOICES
A COLLECTION OF SHORT FICTION

MERLE MOLOFSKY

International Psychoanalytic Books (IPBooks)
New York • IPBooks.net

International Psychoanalytic Books (IPBooks)
Queens, New York
Online at: www.IPBooks.net

Front Cover Image by Xek Noir
Cover Design by Kathy Kovacic of Blackthorn Studio
Dedication Page Photo of Jonathan Molofsky and his shofar by Aideen Nunan
Book Design by Dan Williams

ISBN: 978-1-949093-11-7

Printed in the United States of America

The Creative Spirit

"Mitákuye-Oyás'in"
"All My Relations — We Are All Related"
—Lakota saying, prayer of harmony

I and Thou
—Martin Buber

Amplifying the Voices of Humanity

Sh'ma, I Hear Voices

INTRODUCTION

In this collection of short stories by psychoanalyst, writer and poet Merle Molofsky we are treated to a collection of characters all searching for their personal meaning or, in some cases, their survival. The stories range over different time periods and different settings. In one chapter, a 10-year-old girl and her pregnant mother flee from the ghettos of Eastern Europe and from the endemic anti-Semitism that surrounded them, and Molofsky joins us with her characters as they both yearn to see the tall Lady in New York Harbor. Each narration tells a vibrant tale...most poignantly in how a young girl survives a pre-Roe vs, Wade illegal abortion when society had turned its eyes away in denial of this all too human situation. In "Lazarus", as well as in "Reader, I Married Him", Molofsky explores how one learns to negotiate love and identity, even when one is perhaps just a bit too young and alone to negotiate such life tasks.

Molofsky's range of interest is broad; she goes beyond the everyday life experiences that are the backdrop of most of her stories. For example, in "Danila" she treats us to viewing what it might be like to view our experiences through the lens of timelessness and absence of clear boundaries. Her masterful play between subject and object, on the mystery of before and now, on the singular and the plural... is not only informative but an adventure to read. In "Street Songs" she paints the excitement as well as the everydayness of neighborhood living, with its prejudices and confinements; all of which we have come to accept under the rubric of society's rules. Molofsky goes from a graphic description of the violence of street life in one tale to another in which she invites the reader into the internal personal meanderings of an unhappy and distracted suburban housewife—so subtly that the reader merges with the character as if an unknown part of oneself has been awakened. Calling on our capacity for cross-identification, we are invited to dream along with the protagonist—a magical place—in which dreaming deepens who we are. If one lets it. Molofsky calls this work "What Are Patterns For?"

These tales, written over a period of more than 40 years, reveal a more than probing and informed mind. They reveal a writer who loves and cherishes the human situation—with all our absurdities as well as our triumphs. Molofsky is an insightful writer; she informs and deepens our sensibilities so that we come to know more about life and about ourselves. One cannot ask more from a writer. Molofsky gives us no less.

Gerald J. Gargiulo, PhD

CONTENTS

Chapter One
MIRIAM 1960

December 1960. New York City. Miriam was pregnant and that was her fate. It had always been about to happen and now it was so. Miriam. She was eighteen, unmarried, not in love, born Jewish, and unconscious of being female from the inside out. Promiscuous, what would have been described as a classic textbook nymphomaniac. She menstruated heavily and irregularly, on a cycle that ranged anywhere from 33 to 66 days. Although willing to talk freely about anything she was thinking and feeling, she had never met anyone to whom she was able to talk as freely as she was willing. Thus she never talked to anyone about anything she was feeling and thinking and she didn't know anything at all. When she felt anything immediately and deeply, she put it in the file marked "Later". And what was felt and what was done slipped like running water through laxly laced fingers into the past. Time was a known constant, though of course it was constantly changing everything else. Miriam was pregnant and that was her fate. New York City. December 1960.

As Miriam knew the law of her time and place and station, abortion was illegal, and both the executor of the abortion and the woman who underwent the abortion were guilty of a crime. As Miriam knew the social form of her time and place and station, pregnancy out of wedlock was shameful, barring both the pregnant woman and her family from respect. Miriam, pregnant, considered two choices: 1) that she would approach her parents and confess to them that she was pregnant out of wedlock, and thus a shameful creature who would disgrace them in the eyes of the world; an impossible choice, 2) that she would disappear, leaving behind a note that would claim some crazy young scheme about travel or something, which would distress her parents greatly, while she would enter a home for unwed mothers, have the baby, and give it up for adoption. She settled on the second scheme, without even considering consulting Barry, the young man who had so joyously fathered the baby. Instead, she discussed it with Rob, her closest friend and once-upon-a-time lover. It was Rob who decided when they should be lovers and when they should be friends, a pattern determined by his need to meet and conquer in calculated succession certain cool, full-breasted blondes, during which time Miriam became his confidante and buddy. Rob decided that Miriam's second plan was as unfeasible as her first, that her parents would be terrified and tormented by anxiety if she disappeared, that a note would be no consolation, and that they most likely would trace her to the home she planned to enter. She would thus cause them both anxiety and shame. Besides, those homes cost money. Because Miriam's parents both worked, they managed to tip themselves out of poverty and into the lower middle class, but Miriam, enrolled in one of the city colleges, had no money of her own.

Barry suggested a third possibility, one which Miriam never would have conceived herself. He offered to marry her, thus giving her pregnancy legitimacy, but demanding that after the baby was born that she give up the baby for adoption, as he could not live with a child who was engendered by some other man. As consolation, he suggested that afterward they could have another baby right away. Miriam said no to this third plan.

The reason she said no to the offer of marriage was not a simple reason. She had been in love with this young man before, and could possibly be in love with him again. He was intellectual, passionately immersed in his own emotions and obsessions, and insensitive, even cruel, to her. In fact, he was a type of man with whom she would fall in love over and over again. A man whom, under other conditions, she could have been eagerly persuaded to marry. Her reasons for saying no were: 1) she would have been embarrassed to marry and then give up the baby, as that would have been a clue to its' illicit conception, and 2) once, during a discussion of plans for the future, Rob had said that he needed to marry a doctor's wife, and Miriam knew for sure she would never grow up to be a doctor's wife. and 3) Rob had described the home in which he planned to live when he became a doctor as a white and gold formal fantasy of French provincial furniture and carpeting white and deep as newly-fallen snow, which Miriam knew she could never enjoy and definitely could not keep clean. Miriam had envisioned her future home as full of wooden furniture and unmatched pieces acquired by need and accident, full of people and life.

Those were her reasons, and she said no to the proposal although she always had dreamed of a man wanting to marry her. For a man to want to marry her was her greatest ambition.

Even so, she did not want to marry Rob. He then suggested abortion.

Because abortion was illegal, there was great romance involved in the idea of getting an abortion. What Miriam knew of abortion had been learned from confession magazines and newspaper items. Abortion meant blindfolds, switching from one car to another, mysterious phone calls, I'll be wearing a red carnation, Joe sent me, false names, don't let my mother find out, is this a set-up, what has my body done. There were rumors about the tastes and habits of abortionists, night-time entertainment similar to twice-told tales of the Cropsey maniac and his axe, or Mary, give me back my liver, stories meant to be told by candlelight in a room darkened when summer hurricanes knocked out the electricity. Though there was supposed to be a gentle and understanding doctor practicing in a Pennsylvania backwater who performed abortions at reasonable fees because reportedly his only daughter had died of a back street abortion, and that therefore he never turned a customer away. Later, when Miriam called the number given her by a friend, supposedly the number of the Pennsylvania doctor, a woman's voice told her that the doctor was no longer practicing medicine. Abortions also meant horror stories in the newspapers, complete with every gruesome detail: she died on the operating table, and to avoid scandal the doctor dismembered her and floated parts of her body through the sewage system of Bayonne. After a bungled abortion, her insides were so mangled that she could never have children. Or, knitting needle abortion leads to perforated uterus and death. The smoldering romance of the forbidden. Like drinking in bars, even though you were underage. Or smoking pot. Or making love because you wanted to, even though you weren't married or even engaged, and didn't want or expect to be. Romance.

Miriam decided to get an abortion.

There were two preliminary steps to getting an abortion. An abortionist had to be found, and the fee had to be scraped together.

Miriam lived at home with her parents. Though their combined incomes allowed the family to edge into the lower middle class, there was never any extra money for anything. Miriam had never had new school outfits, movie money, ice cream soda money. She had an allowance that covered her double carfare to school and school lunches. Sixty cents a day to take two busses to and from school, and another forty cents a day to buy cottage cheese and canned fruit platters in the school cafeteria. Another thirty cents for cigarettes. Twenty cents for a drink, coffee or soda. It would have taken Miriam about 30 weeks to save every penny, walk to school, skip lunch, and buy an abortion from the cheapest source. She had no job, no skills, and no expectations. Yet suddenly the fee became easy. Since Miriam was the one who was going to undergo the physical struggle of an abortion, the boy with whom she was having sex gallantly offered to pay for the abortion. He belonged to a house plan, which was a poor boy's fraternity, an organization in which young men from the local college paid monthly dues toward the rental of a few rooms in a basement or over a store near the college campus, but not the expensive initiation fees that fraternities required. The members of the house plan took a good-natured view of the little problems their friends and brothers faced, and amid much conviviality and beer-drinking they held a house plan fund raising drive for Miriam's abortion, and Barry brought her, flushed with beer and camaraderie and success, three hundred dollars in singles, fives, and one twenty dollar bill that he had thrown into the hat himself. Three hundred dollars. And that was it. There was no more money to be found anywhere.

Miriam began to ask around for an abortionist. It seemed to her as if life happened only under thickly quilted, smothering wraps. She wandered around in a world guided sternly by primly plastic rules, a cardboard cut-out world where everybody was a sleek surface of skin, and nothing ever happened. Yet there was life beneath the thin overlay of personality. Everything that was so perfumed, powdered, and polished had an underside, and that underside was beginning to gleam raw and slimy in the uncaring air. People had a self on the inside, and a life that remained hidden, and an underlying stratum of society that existed to intercept the secret life within. Every young woman in college who would admit to not being a convent-raised virgin knew an abortionist or knew of another young woman who knew of an abortionist. The search for the illicit was easily satisfied. Miriam was not as alone as the world had seemed to imply in the drawing back of skirts, the pale prissy rules. Miriam was not alone.

Abortionists began to blossom in the granite of greater New York City. Manhattan, Staten Island, New Jersey, Connecticut, the Virgin Islands.... The first abortionist that Miriam heard of was a medical doctor, male, fifty-five years old, and charged nine hundred dollars. Impossible. The next abortionist Miriam was told about was a medical doctor, male, forty-seven, and asked seven hundred and fifty dollars. Another medical doctor, thirty-eight years old, eight hundred. Another, nine hundred. Another, twelve hundred. Another, five hundred, in the Virgin Islands. A cheapie, who did not come with a high recommendation, six hundred dollars.

The three hundred dollars shriveled into a lump of cold white ash in Miriam's heart. What would it buy?

Her friend Rob had a sister, Irene, who was married to a wealthy and influential young lawyer. She had found the birth of her first and only child, a girl, painful and disappointing. She had not wanted pain, and she had wanted a boy. In some inner logic of her own the pain and the disappointment were intimately entwined. A boy would never have caused her so much pain. She refused to raise the child herself, and her husband paid for a hired nurse. Irene grew fat and lonely. When she found herself pregnant again, her husband paid for an abortion.

"Listen, Miriam, it doesn't have to be expensive to be good. They'll only try to gyp you. You think a grand, or twelve hundred, it's a good doctor? They're all the same, after a certain price. You're paying for their fancy address, for their nurse's beauty parlor bills. Go to this doctor. I know him, I went. Listen, I could afford more, plenty more, believe me. Why pay for what you're not getting? This man is excellent, he knows what he's doing. He's not Fifth Avenue, but it's a nice place, clean, and all my friends go. He's wonderful."

The abortionist charged six hundred dollars for married women, three hundred for single women, a sliding scale that was evidence, Irene went on to say, of his compassion and sensitivity to the needs of women facing unwanted pregnancies. The tone in which she said this was as flat and cheerful as if she were saying, unwanted facial hair. The doctor's offices were in Teaneck, New Jersey. Miriam was to call, tell him that she was recommended by Mrs. Harold Stern, and to say she was suffering from a skin infection, the code word for pregnancy.

The receptionist answering the phone did not sound friendly. She asked, crisply, for Miriam to give her name again. Miriam stuttered through the unfamiliar syllables, feeling the lie reveal itself in the secret sounds of her voice, the amateur flaccidity of her tongue. Mary Harding. My name is Mary Harding. The receptionist, once again, asked in an even more sour tone, what the ailment seemed to be. A skin infection. Miriam scratched at a sudden attacking itch at her left ankle and wondered whether god indeed was punishing her for lying. And who had recommended her? Mrs. Harold Stern. The receptionist claimed never to have heard of Mrs. Harold Stern. It was the only true part of the dialogue, and it was being doubted. Miriam didn't know what to say.

"Listen," Miriam said. "I don't know what to say. Mrs. Stern told me that she was treated by the doctor."

"What for?"

"For a skin infection. She said she was his patient. I don't know what to say. She recommended him."

"I see. And you have a skin infection too."

"Yes."

"Well, we have no record of any Mrs. Harold Stern. What's her first name?"

"Irene. Her name is Irene Stern."

"Checking. We have no record of any Mrs. Stern, not even an Irene Stern. There is no patient by that name. You must have called the wrong doctor."

"Wait a minute, "Miriam pleaded, clutching at the phone. "I don't know what to say." Miriam felt as if she were drowning. "I know she gave me this number."

"I will check our files again. Call back in ten minutes."

A dead and shriveled phone. Miriam waited and called back.

"Yes, our records do show that we treated a Mrs. Harold Stern. What did you say your name was?"

"Mary," Miriam said. "Mary Harding."

"We have only one opening. Wednesday afternoon at three thirty. If you are late you will not be seen by the doctor. Mrs. Stern told you our fees. You must have the entire amount in cash with you or the doctor will not be able to see you."

Miriam had six days to wait. On what she felt was the spur of the moment, she went to a beauty parlor for the third time of her life and had her hair dyed black, to make her look older, more sophisticated. In the close and clammy heat, under the blast of the hair dryer, she fainted. It was for Miriam proof that she really was pregnant. Until then, the four months of missed periods, two missed periods, and a rabbit test, had been the only, and to Miriam, inconclusive signs of pregnancy. She hadn't felt pregnant. She had had no morning sickness, no tenderness of breasts, and did not expect a weight gain. Nothing had happened to her. Now, the fainting made the pregnancy and the doctor's conclusion a reality. It wasn't an imaginary pregnancy and she wasn't going to have an imaginary abortion.

Barry borrowed a friend's car and drove her to New Jersey on Wednesday. He was not permitted to come into the office with her. No one was. On the way there was very little either of them wanted to say. Miriam kept touching her hair nervously, as if she could feel the slick blank blackness curling over her tentative fingers. Rob had said that she looked like a tramp, and Barry said she didn't look like herself. Miriam thought she looked like a tramp and that she really looked like herself. There was no real way to tell that to anyone. She felt old in her hair and as young as the unformed fear laboring in her womb. She felt as if she were about to give birth to terror, or have her last trace of childhood yanked from between her legs sometime that afternoon. Barry asked her if she had had any lunch.

"I couldn't eat."

"Yeah, I guess not. Maybe I'll get something while I'm waiting.

There must be a diner around."

They ran into traffic on the bridge. Though they had started out early enough to enable them to arrive half an hour early, the unexpected traffic slowed them down, and they arrived exactly on time. There was no time for hand holding, whispers of encouragement, confession of fear. Miriam didn't want to look at the clean damp bones of his cheeks, or the unthinking arch of his lips, or the little beads of oil at his hairline. Hatred flooded her, starting at the navel and oozing into her thighs. She wanted to cut something forever limp and dead out of him, but she didn't know exactly what. As she ran from the car to the office, her pale skin began to take on a faint rose tinge in the sharp winter air.

Miriam recognized the receptionist by her voice. "Mary Harding? I don't believe we have an appointment for anyone with that name."

"I called last week. Mrs. Harold Stern referred me."

"Mrs. Harold Stern? The doctor doesn't have any patient by that name."

"Look, I came all the way from Brooklyn—"

"Our patients come from all over the world. The doctor is a noted doctor. And we never see anyone without an appointment and a recommendation."

"Well, I did call and I did make an appointment and Mrs. Stern did refer me."

"I'll check again, but I really do not remember making an appointment with anyone with the name of what? Mary what?"

"Mary Harding."

"Mary Harding. Harding. No, I don't see— Oh, here it is. What are you doing tucked in under here? Harding. Miss or Mrs.?"

"Miss."

"Oh. I see. You're not married."

"No."

"Have a seat, Mary. The doctor will see you shortly."

The other women in the office were older, well-dressed, distant. Their faces were smooth and high, like well-planed rocky peaks that were cloven and polished by turmoil and wind. There was no one there whom Mary recognized by the warmth in the center of their eyes. Their eyeballs were blank, almost colorless, like Grecian statuary. No one seemed to see her at all.

Miriam shrank into the wall. She became another rosebud on the baroque vine of fantasy flora within the wallpaper. She waited for the doctor to see her shortly for about two hours and twenty-three minutes. Since she had been cautioned to come to the office alone and not to let anybody at all know where she was, she was afraid to leave and tell Barry to be patient. She hoped he hadn't panicked and left, or gone to the police. She hoped he had gotten his lunch at some diner. She forgot how much she hated the shape of the pores of his nose, the pimple she knew was forming on his left shoulder, his moist melodic laughter. She worried about him. And she read magazines she would never have dreamed of reading, magazines of worlds she did not recognize and of which she knew nothing, Vogue and Harper's and The New Yorker. She liked the cartoons in The New Yorker, but she did not laugh aloud. "Mary Harding." The name meant nothing to her. She did not look up.

Impatiently, "Mary Harding. If there is no one here by that name, I will call the next patient."

Miriam jumped up, and the magazine she had been reading slid from her lap to the carpet. She bent down to pick it up, dropped it once more, and followed the scornful back of the receptionist into the back rooms of the office, encased in a flaming sweat born of embarrassment and fear.

The doctor was unusually small, perhaps five feet even, with crooked shoulders, wire-rim glasses, grey cheeks, and bleached hands. His distended blue veins looked spongy, insubstantial, about to dissolve in the arid whiteness of his flesh. She sat facing him across his huge blonde wood desk, seeing nothing but his magnified eyes swimming like tadpoles with moist and crazy motion behind his think distorting lenses. "What's the matter?"

"I'm pregnant."

"You think you're pregnant. How do you know?"

"I went to the doctor. He took tests."

"So why did you think you were pregnant?"

"I missed two periods." She did not say that two periods for her meant four months.

"What do you want me to do about it?"

"I don't want to have a baby."

"Why not?"

"I'm not married."

"So get married."

"There's no one to marry."

"Hmmm. You're pregnant and you're not married and you don't want to have a baby. What am I supposed to tell you. You shouldn't have gotten pregnant."

"I know." She is very ashamed. "But I am."

"Hmmm. How many boys are there? One? More?"

"One."

"You make love, he has intercourse? You do nothing else?"

"What do you mean?"

"I mean, you don't touch each other with the hands, or do something with the mouth? How does he touch you? You touch him with your hands?"

"I can't talk about it."

"You should, you'd learn how not to get pregnant. You should learn. I could teach you. How old are you?"

"Eighteen." She is telling the truth. Why should she be lying. But her face is soft and round, her lips do not remain closed, but part like a sleeping infant's lips part; her breath seems young, pre-verbal. Short, Mediterranean, dark-eyed, uncreased, with a straight waist and small breasts, she looks 15, perhaps 16. She looks very very young.

"I could show you how not to get pregnant, but still have a nice time with your boyfriend. But you are too young for all of this." The doctor frowns. "Too young. You would tell someone. I cannot help you about this baby. You have to go somewhere else. You would get frightened or feel bad and you would tell someone. Your mother, perhaps, or an aunt. A girlfriend. Too young. You have to be at least 21."

"But why?" Miriam stood up, her voice strained, low, pleading. "Oh, please. I promise I won't tell anybody. I don't want my mother to find out. I won't tell her. Oh, please, I'm desperate. Please."

"No. Too young. Look, little girl, this is a serious business. I could lose my license, my livelihood, go to jail. What if you became ill? If you didn't follow instructions, and did something stupid, something wrong? What would you do? You would tell your mother. Too young. I only treat married women." He opened the door. She had nothing to do but leave.

Barry jumped to his feet when he saw her coming. He had been leaning against the car, despite the cold, and chain-smoking, though he seldom smoked. He reached out a hand to touch her cheek and his touch was so cold her cheek felt numb.

"Are you all right?"

"No."

"Baby, what's wrong? What happened?"

"Nothing. I'm too young."

"What do you mean?"

"He wouldn't do it. He said I was too young,"

The ride home was filled with automatic music from the car radio. Miriam sensed Barry not as another human being but as some gelatinous ooze; he was too dense, too close, too fearful. She felt that if she did not get away from him and his too young voice edged with unnamed fear, from his body lithe and athletic and yet somehow coagulated into an unmovable thickness, from his clean hair and tense eyes and reeky maleness, she would hate him forever. He would have to be human alone, without her. She fled into silence. It was as familiar as the rest of her life, her silence. She knew that she would never want to see him again. She did not want to touch him or smell him. He choked her. She was grateful for his money. Her body settled down, became lead.

Three weeks later a friend of hers met her in the cafeteria on campus. Good news. She had a phone number. Miriam could now get the abortion she had always wanted to have. She called the number. A man answered.

"Sandra told me to tell you that she gave this phone number to me. It's about that job as a waitress."

"Yeah, the job as a waitress. Sandra gave you the address?"

"Uh, no, she didn't. Uh, she said you would give it to me."

"Yeah, right. Listen, you have to come here all alone. Don't let nobody even drive you around the corner. All alone. If you don't come all alone, no job. You understand?"

"Yeah. Yeah, sure."

"Oh, and bring that one hundred fifty deposit for your uniform, you know what I mean?"

"Yeah. Sure."

He gave her the time and the address. Thursday at 1:45 pm. Miriam found the apartment building, a narrow six-story corner building of dark red brick, fronted by a faded green canopy and equally faded doorman, incongruously set on the edge of a tenement block on the Lower East Side. Miriam asked for Mr. Todd and the elevator operator took her to the fourth floor. The apartment was a studio apartment in the rear, cheerlessly lit through a northern window facing an airshaft. The layout of the apartment was cramped and narrow, with a miniature stainless steel and birch kitchen set into an alcove, with a modest mess of breakfast dishes and wine glasses from the night before. The single room left was dominated by an impersonally modern bar and stereo, a day bed covered with beige corduroy, and a case full of unmemorable recordings. Too many strings were turning a bland popular song into soup, too loudly.

Mr. Todd was in his late thirties, balding, overweight, with a wide bottom and ponderous thighs, dressed in a short-sleeved shirt, although it was late December, almost Christmas, a yellow tie, and plaid pants. As Miriam entered the tiny entrance foyer he touched her at the elbow, guiding her toward the daybed.

"So you're pregnant."

"Yes." The apartment was overheated. Miriam began to feel something she wasn't to recognize, identify, or ever act upon until years later. The feeling was panic. She wanted to get out, as if she were in a stuck elevator, or a sinking ship, or caught between pit and pendulum.

"You know, you're not going to be able to make love for quite a while after this little operation. Want to get in a final quick one before we leave for the place?" Mr. Todd was grinning at her, a cigarette flying like a smoking flag in his mouth. His eyes remained on her face, on her mouth.

"No." She felt frozen. She may have felt fear.

"Well, lots of girls like to make a little love before they go through with this. It'll be your last chance for a couple of weeks. Don't lose out on a good thing now. I was just trying to do you a favor. You could make love now without rubbers or anything, you know, because you can't get pregnant. That's a joke." He waited for her to laugh. She didn't. "Look, I'm not going to rape you, relax. Don't get upset. I never hurt anyone in my whole life. I got all the girls I want. I got money, see, and girls like money. I just thought you'd like a little before we left, that's all. Want a drink? It'll loosen you up."

"No."

Mr. Todd grabbed a car coat that was lying on a chair. "Okay, doll, let's go. You got the money?"

Miriam nodded.

"Better give it to me now." Miriam handed over to him the hundred and fifty dollars in ones and fives and one twenty. He counted it twice.

"You got a deal, you know. This is very cheap. When you think about it, part of it is for me and part of this is for the nurse who's going to do this. That's not very much, right? I bet you heard lots of places that want four, five, six hundred dollars. Look, some places even charge a grand, twelve, fourteen hundred. And for what? For nothing. This is a very simple little operation. Look, you're getting a bargain. Relax. Nothing's going to happen to you. Why you doing this, huh? Didn't the guy want to marry you?"

"I don't want to get married."

"You don't? Don't give me that. Every girl wants to get married. He just didn't want to marry you, right? Look, don't feel so bad. He's probably too young to get married. He's probably not even out of school yet. He's got a whole life to lead. You'll meet some one older, more settled, you'll get married. If I were a little younger, ha ha, I'd marry you myself. Can you cook?"

Miriam didn't answer.

"Just a joke, just a joke." They walked out of the building and toward a car. "Listen, if you don't want to marry this guy, how come you didn't want to make love while we were upstairs? I mean, honey, you're no virgin, I know that." Miriam sat motionless in the car as Mr. Todd drove and talked. She had nothing to say.

"What's the matter, cat got your tongue? Look, I don't mean to upset you. I'm no rapist or molester, you know. Look, I didn't even touch you. Relax. Nervous, huh? First time abortion, right? Relax. Mrs. Sanchez has done hundreds of these things. She even did my sister. You'll love her. She's a very nice woman. You got nothing to worry about. Everything's going to be all right. I bet you wish you had done it back at my place. Last chance, you know. A couple of weeks with no loving gets pretty hard, especially at your age, especially when you get used to getting it regular. You're used to getting it, I bet." They were moving up the FDR Drive. Mr. Todd was a careful, alert driver. He chain smoked as he drove. Miriam felt a feeling she barely acknowledged. It began with a drumming within her stomach, her chest, a fluttering beating of a message she was not going to heed: get out of here, get out of here, get out of here. Give it up. Turn back. Stop. Fins on life. Do over. You don't have to do this. As usual, Miriam didn't pay any attention to the feeling or the message, the fear, the panic. She knew she had to do this. It was her fate. She deserved it. There was nothing else to do.

Mrs. Sanchez lived on 155th Street, in an enormous bank of tenement that stretched a long long city block and looked like a medieval fortress. The courtyard was rank with a hundred forgotten acts that left behind scents like ghosts. Miriam and Mr. Todd walked up to the fifth floor. At the end of a narrow unlit foyer six small children were gathered in a drape-darkened living room, warming themselves before the blue fire of a TV set. Mrs. Sanchez, small, round, bustling, bobbing, ushered them in to a tiny room off the hall. It was empty save for a doctor's examining table with stirrups, a stool, and a rickety table on which were placed a number of surgical appliances upon the exposed metal table top. Mr. Todd sat down on the stool to watch. Mrs. Sanchez closed the door. The slick black and white noises of a cartoon fight slithered through the breathing pores of the walls.

During the entire preparation and procedure Mrs. Sanchez talked on in a cheerful, reassuring babble. "I've done this thousands of times. My oldest daughter has had five abortions already from me, so you can tell I know what I'm doing. If I didn't know what I was doing, I wouldn't give her five abortions now, would I? Five abortions and nothing happened, nothing went wrong. All her friends come to me too. The whole neighborhood comes to me. I'm a licensed nurse, you know, a licensed practical nurse. I know this kind of stuff inside and out. Listen, honey, I'm telling you what I'm doing so you'll know what to expect and what's going to happen and everything, so you can take care of things yourself without making mistakes. All right?"

Miriam nodded. She had removed her panties but left on her garter belt, though she had unsnapped her stockings and had rolled them down around her ankles. Lying flat on her back with her legs spread and placed in stirrups, she was treated to a view of her rolled down stockings and scuffed two inch black pumps. Her legs looked raw and plucked in the dim light. She could see the dark pinpoints where hair had begun to grow back from the scraping shaving of her legs. Her skirt was pushed up high, and bunched around her waist. Mr. Todd's breathing seemed as thick as syrup in the small dark room.

"All right, I'm going to strap you down. You look like a brave girl. You're not going to kick or anything, right? It hurts a teeny bit for only a second or two, but some girls, you know, they kick and scream and kick around as if I was coming at them with a knife. I done this to my daughter five times, remember? Okay. Now all

I'm doing is cleaning you with a little alcohol, so it might sting a little. It's nothing. Okay. Now I'm not going to clean you out, scrape you or anything, because you only missed two periods. I'm going to give you a needle, like an injection right into the womb where the baby is, that the baby won't like because I'm giving it salt, and the baby can't hold on inside if there's salt, so he's going to have to come out. Now that won't happen for a long time. The salt has to work first." Between her legs and into her insides in places that she had never felt anything at all Miriam now felt a long sour pain, a wrenching and burning that began achingly and peaked to a needle-like flaming howl from the inside out. Tears splashed over the stern and delicate membrane of her tensing eyes, but she made no sound, not even a moan.

"Oh good, you're a good brave girl. That's why I make the TV so loud, in case a girl might scream. I don't want the neighbors to call the cops or anything, if they think someone's being murdered or something. It'll just last a few more minutes now." The pain stayed on a thin even silver arc, and then receded in long swooping gulps.

"There, that's done. It's all over. In a minute now you'll be able to take your legs down and go home. Now, while you're resting, I'll give you some instructions. Later tonight you are going to pass some blood and like a spongy small thing all wrapped in the blood. That's the fetus, the baby. It's almost like a period, like the curse. Don't use a tampon, though, use a napkin, or you'll get an infection. You might get some cramps, like with your period. That's all. If in a day the bleeding don't stop, then something went wrong, you're not healthy or something, I don't know. It hardly ever happens, you understand, but I have to tell you about it, warn you, you know, in case it does happen and you're not healthy like you look, you could die if I don't tell you. Then you go to the doctor but you tell him you just gave birth, you don't tell him you had an AB and of course you never mention my name. It's best you forget my name, if you know what I mean. If you tell them you had an AB they'll put you in jail when you get healthy again, because you broke the law. Don't tell them nothing."

Miriam's legs were removed from the stirrups, and she stood up, pulling her skirt down. Mr. Todd got up and went into the hallway, pattering down the hallway to catch a last look at the TV set. Miriam slid shakily from the table, the memory of pain sloshing weakly at her ankles and knees, so that she couldn't stand without tottering. She leaned against the table while she put on her panties and fixed her stockings. Mrs. Sanchez watched her impatiently, her flat dark eyes puckering. "You're going to be fine. No more baby, no more troubles. Believe me, no more baby is what's important. You shouldn't be tied down with a baby at your age. You should have a little fun first, before you get stuck in the house with babies. And if you ever need me again, you come back here." She dropped her voice, leaned over almost lasciviously, and whispered, "Remember my address when you leave. If you ever need me again, come straight to me. Don't call that Mr. Todd. What do you want to mess with a man like him for. He's no good."

"You look all right." Mr. Todd patted Miriam's shoulder as they walked down the stairs. "No problem, right? If most men knew what I knew, they wouldn't be all worried about women the way they are. Look at you, you just had an AB and you're bounding down the stairs like you just came from your boyfriend's bed. Listen," he added worriedly as he saw her twisting back to look at the building, "You better forget this place, forget the address, forget her name. You don't know her, you don't know nothing. Listen, if anything goes wrong, don't get her in trouble. She has kids to feed. She does a lot of good in this world, helping girls like you out of trouble. If you tell a doctor you had an AB, they'll put you in jail. It's a criminal act, getting an abortion." Mr. Todd whispered the last few sentences, slipping a finger under his collar and easing it, as if it were all of a sudden too tight. They drove down back along the FDR Drive in silence.

Miriam leaned her head against the glass pane of the car window, feeling comforted by the smooth impersonality and iciness of its touch. The landscape was unfamiliar to her in the quasi-darkness of city night, and the dazzle of lights along the water seemed eerie, almost threatening. As if the world were a big Christmas package, and there was nothing left to give except death. Mr. Todd had not even driven past a subway station, but had driven directly back to his apartment building. "Want to come up and rest a while?"

Miriam shook her head no, and started to wander away toward the subway. "Don't forget to call us if you ever need us again. Tell your friends about us. You might need me again some day," Mr. Todd called out to Miriam's crouched back.

Miriam went straight to Rob's house. He had offered to spend the evening with her, to help her if she needed help, to support her if she needed support. He seemed surprised to see her.

"You all right? Everything okay?"

"Yes. I just have to wait a few hours. I'm afraid to wait alone. Can I wait here?"

"Sure. Listen, I can't spend much time with you, though. My friend from school is here. Fred. Did you ever meet him? Anyway, he's got a report due tomorrow on *The Brothers Karamazov* and I'm helping him with it. He really doesn't have any good ideas about it at all, and you know how much I love that book. You read it. We used to talk about it all the time."

Yes, Miriam had read it too. No, she didn't want to help. "Can't I just sit in the same room with you? I won't make any noise. It's not all over yet and I'm afraid to go home."

"Yeah, sure. Sure, kid. I just won't be able to talk to you much, okay?"

Was it okay? Miriam seemed to remember that Rob had promised to spend this evening with her, to help her through. It was as if he had forgotten. As if he hadn't thought it was important. Miriam didn't want to feel that feeling, think that thought. So she stopped. Fred had a paper due that next morning. It was very important. Miriam knew she had no right to expect anything. She knew what she had done, the kind of girl she was. She felt anger, but she pushed it away, saved it for later. For much later. She couldn't be angry now. What she wanted she wasn't going to get. It didn't matter.

"Look, Fred," Rob was arguing, his cheeks glowing pinkly with evening lamplight and the excitement of the literary hunt, "You can't claim that Dostoevsky was wrong about good and evil and god and stuff. Your job isn't to argue with the writer, your job is to analyze the work."

"Yeah, but I have a right to think, don't I," Fred responded, somewhat sulkily. He did not share the same fervor for literature as did Rob and Miriam, and once he had conceived of an idea he was reluctant to let it go. "And I think this guy couldn't think his way out of a paper bag. He's too narrow-minded. He didn't understand anything about the real world."

"How can you say that!" Rob cried, his voice twisting dryly. "You don't know what you're talking about." Rob smote his forehead with his hand and paced up and down the room, obviously distressed. "What Dostoevsky knew about the human soul.... Fred, he was the greatest psychologist that ever lived. Look, ask Miriam... she's talked about this with me hundreds of times. Miriam, tell Fred about what your teacher said about Dostoevsky understanding women better than any woman writer ever could."

Miriam, overcome by a rush of feelings she knew she wasn't supposed to feel, had nothing to say. A tremble of self-pity masked a deeper, murderous rage. She was unaware that her neck and shoulder muscles were tensing, like a cat getting ready to spring. She concentrated instead on suppressing the more familiar rush of tears. Later she would have a stiff neck, and think it was from standing in a draft. And shame at feeling even her quickly muted anger caused her to apologize. "I can't help you, Rob. I'm really sorry, but I don't really feel well."

"Oh, yeah, sure, I forgot. That's okay. You just rest, kid." Rob flipped through his copy of the book, looking for the passage he felt would finally convince Fred.

"The trouble with Dostoevsky," Fred persisted, "is that he thinks good and evil are possible, and that's why he's wrong!" Fred's voice took on the triumphant sound of brass. "Admit it, Rob, admit it! He thinks there is such a thing as good and evil, and that's why he's wrong."

Rob cudgeled his brows with both fists. "Look, dummy, I don't have to admit anything. It doesn't matter if he was right or wrong. What matters is how he used the structure of the novel to present his ideas, how his characters and their lives enact the moral conflicts. The ideas don't count at all. Do you understand?"

Miriam looked up at Rob, startled. She had never heard him deny the importance of Dostoevsky's ideas before. The ideas were important to her because they were important to Rob. "Rob, do you believe what you're saying?"

Rob jerked his head toward her, irritated. "The ideas aren't important that way, not for the paper he's writing, that's all I mean. Listen, Miriam, if you're not going to help with the paper, don't interrupt, okay?"

Miriam sank back down onto Rob's bed. "Okay."

The argument dribbled on for hours. The paper was being slowly constructed, Rob outlining the major line of argument on blue-lined legal-size yellow paper as they talked. Rob's mother brought in a tray of iced tea and tuna salad sandwiches on rye bread. "Oh, Miriam?" Her voice was surprised, questioning. "I didn't know you were here. Are you hungry, darling?"

"No, Mrs. Goldman. Thank you very much."

"You young girls today are all the same. Skinny as toothpicks, and always dieting. You should eat."

"Ma, she's not hungry."

"It's not healthy. A girl should have some meat on her bones." Mrs. Goldman crept closer into the room, and craned her neck to see the mystery and importance being written in block letters by her son. Rob covered the pad with his fist. "I said she's not hungry. Will you leave her alone? Look, we're working. Go inside." Mrs. Goldman shuffled out of the room, her swollen feet inside her pink mules making sliding sounds of resentment as her mouth apologized.

Miriam dozed.

"Then what does that incident mean, Rob?" Fred's voice was growing shrill. The half inch of iced tea left in his glass had grown lukewarm. "When that story about the serf boy being torn to pieces by dogs in front of his mother's eyes, by orders of the landowner, is told by Ivan, it's obvious that anyone with any sense could see that if this world were created by a god, he wasn't a just god. And, in fact, a thing like that couldn't be created by anyone at all except a devil. But a devil couldn't create all the good and beautiful things either. So Ivan is right, and Dostoevsky knows it, but doesn't have the courage to admit it, even to himself."

"Then why did he crack up at the end?" Rob asked truculently, his blue eyes bloodshot, his fat golden-haired fist carving one last note onto the page.

"Because the truth that there is no god is too much for the intellect to bear!" Fred shouted. "The world is full of horror! And Dostoevsky's precious faith is just a fairy tale to cover up the horror."

"That's exactly what your paper is going to prove!" Rob shouted triumphantly. "God created the intellect to be subservient to faith."

Miriam stirred from the bed, swung her legs over, and sat up. "Maybe god created the world so that we could never understand it. Book of Job." To mitigate the remark, she smiled.

"Want to hear a joke?" Fred asked, flopping down on the bed next to Miriam.

"Yeah." Rob looked up expectantly, needing to be amused. On the crest of his thin upper lip blond hairs glistened. Miriam tried to smile some more, but the fade-away of her last smile lingered, her lips were stiff, and she couldn't feel any feelings at all.

"Okay," Fred smirked. "It seems that a message in skywriting in all the world's different languages appeared, announcing that god was going to appear in the Vatican in three days, and expected all the world's religious leaders to attend. Well, preparations were made, and at the end of the three days all the world's religious leaders appeared at the Vatican, along with swarms of people eager to get a glimpse of god. So finally a green flying saucer space ship appeared in the sky and landed right in the middle of the Vatican courtyard. So out of the space ship come all these angels, all dressed in white robes, with glittering wings and halos and crap, and the head angel says that god wants to see the pope first, that the pope should come into the space ship. You can imagine the scene, right, with all the hysterical crying people, people in wheelchairs crying, 'I'm cured! I'm cured!', with heavenly trumpets."

"Yeah, yeah, yeah," Rob interrupted. "Get to the point."

"All right. So the pope goes into the space ship and stays there a whole hour, with everyone all wondering what was happening and that crap. Finally the pope comes out with this look of awe on his face, completely carried away. Everyone rushes up to him and starts to ask, 'Well, what does god look like?' and crap. The pope mops his brow, takes a deep breath, and says, 'Well, first of all, she's colored.'"

Rob cracked up. He rolled on the floor, gripping his stomach and laughing, wheezing over and over again, "She's colored, she's colored". Miriam politely, in confusion, also laughed.

"Listen, Rob," Miriam murmured, when he caught his breath, "It's almost one in the morning. I have to get home. Are you almost finished?"

"No, just with the outline. Now we have to write the paper."

"Well, can't Fred write the paper? It's all outlined now and everything."

Rob looked disgusted. "What do you want? You know I told you I'd help him with it. This is the hard part."

"Well, can you and Fred drive me home? I'm afraid to take the subway. I have cramps. They've been happening for about an hour now."

"Oh Jesus. I told you— Okay, all right. We'll do something. You know, Fred has to have this paper by nine o'clock tomorrow morning, typed and everything."

"But you knew I was coming over. You told me to."

"Yeah, but I thought you'd be leaving earlier. I thought you could get home yourself. You always do. Listen, can you take a cab?"

"I don't have any money."

"Don't be ridiculous. We'll give you money. I'll call a cab."

In anger, with a grimly distracted look on his face, Rob phoned for a cab. Miriam stood in the hallway, buttoning her coat. Voices drifted to her from Rob's open bedroom door.

"Okay, Fred, so the first page is where you're going to sketch out the basic premise. Now, according to the outline, the basic premise is that although Ivan is intellectually correct, he does not possess the whole truth—"

"But he does!"

"You're not listening. I'm not finished. He does not possess the whole truth according to Dostoevsky! That's your basic premise, the thesis you're going to develop. Look, let's write it down."

"But Rob, you're not leaving any space for my opinions."

"Your opinions come in the end."

"Oh."

Rob's mother, her floating panels of beige nightgown covered by a quilted robe, came padding into the hallway. "Miriam? You're still here? It's so late. Your mother is going to be worried."

"Mrs. Goldman. I was just leaving. It was an interesting discussion. I got very involved."

"You don't look well. You look tired. You know what they say, a girl should get her beauty sleep."

The cab ride home was longer than Miriam had imagined. The ten dollar bill shoved into her hand by Rob felt stiff and hot and aggressive. It was money. At home, Miriam slept. Nothing had happened. The cramps were barely noticeable.

At eight o'clock in the morning Miriam awoke to severe cramps. She was bleeding heavily. This is it, she thought, a groggy hangover of sleep leveling her fear. Oh, I hope my mother leaves the house soon. Her mother came into her bedroom. "Miriam, I'm leaving. Aren't you getting up?"

"I have my period. I don't feel well."

"Nonsense. If you get up you'll feel much better. Don't stay in bed all morning. Get up and go for a walk." At eight fifteen the front door slammed. Her mother had left for work. Miriam got up and groped her way from bed to the kitchen. Normally she could eat or drink nothing in the morning. Food, she said, made her feel too nervous. But this morning her throat felt scratchy, parched, as if she had swallowed a cupful of burning sand. She drank a glass of water. The cramps intensified and she crept back into bed.

By ten that morning she lay huddled beneath blankets damp from sweat, weeping. The pains had become so intense that she could barely breathe. They became rhythmical threatening angry waves, lifting her up as if a strong arm had gathered her at the waist, then slamming her down, as if she were a leaf in a rising gale of pain. She felt a strange sensation in her pelvis, as if she were a nut being squeezed in a giant nutcracker. Within she felt a bone-crunching massive block of pain, squeezing in upon her and bursting out in a simultaneous wrench. In a demented panic she ran into the bathroom, clutching at her middle, and squatted upon the white tile floor, her head lolling against the smooth cold full- length mirror on the door. She saw leaning against the mirror, from the other side of cold, a girl with disheveled black hair and a tensely contorted face, a girl like herself, but frozen, preserved under glass. Safe. Distant. The cracking pain repeated, and she delivered, among a gush of water and blood, a tiny blue fetus, perfectly formed, with miniature fingernails, puckered shut eyelids, tiny nipples on swollen breasts, delicate folds of vulva, strained bow of mouth, frail shoulders and thighs, dimpled clenched fists. It lay in the mess on the cold tile floor, very dead, while Miriam sat back and stared in a pale horror at the little blue baby still connected to her beating heart. She stared at the baby and she stared at the girl in the mirror staring back at her, a girl connected with a little dead baby, but behind glass, where there was no heartbeat, no sound.

What could she do? She knew nothing at all of birth. She knew nothing of her own body, loathed everything about her body except the allowable outer surface of skin, of dead cells arranged in configurations of hair and nails. Lurking beneath the tangled dark hair of her vulva was, she dimly knew, something else, another mouth, perhaps, wet and lewd and not to be touched or seen or thought about. And from there this blue horror had come. She knew nothing at all of birth.

Miriam had not even seen a movie in a high school "hygiene" class. But she had read, in some novel, perhaps, a novel set in a New Zealand sheep farm or some rugged Scottish moor, about animals biting off the umbilical cord. You have to cut the cord, she thought, you have to cut the cord. Electrical impulses inside her brain beat a numb refrain against her sweat-soaked forehead. You have to cut the cord.

Although she had not yet delivered the placenta, for Miriam did not know about the placenta, she found the shears used for trimming her bangs, and cut the cord. She did not tie it. And the great artery that connected the dead baby's life with hers began to pump away her blood, and she did not know it.

The pains grew worse. She tried to wrap the dead baby in toilet paper, used practically a whole roll, and then wrapped the baby in a towel. With another towel she cleaned up the mess on the floor, and dumped the sticky burden in the garbage. The pains grew worse. She felt dizzy. The walls tipped, the furniture reeled. She stuffed another towel between her legs to stop the bleeding. She grabbed for the phone, knocked over the telephone stand, with its notepads and pencils and ashtray, called the operator, and asked for a hospital. "Please, I'm bleeding. I'm bleeding all over."

An ambulance, constructed in the shape of a square and bouncing creakily, arrived from the city hospital. The attendants refused to take her when they saw her and asked her age. She was, they said, only eighteen, and therefore a legal minor. "You have to be twenty-one, Miss. We can't take you. We need your parents' consent."

"Please. I'm bleeding. It hurts. Please. I won't sue you."

Miriam crawled back to the phone. The ambulance attendants refused to touch her, to help her move, because she was not yet twenty-one. She called her mother at work, only a few blocks away. Her mother rushed home. The ambulance attendants placed Miriam between their ridged arms, in a hand carry, and bore her down to the ambulance. Her mother did not know what was wrong, but had given frightened consent with one glimpse of Miriam's drained face. All the neighbors came out to watch. No one knew what had happened. Miriam's face, white with lack of blood, gleamed against the artificial shadow of her hair. She looked like a black and white photograph of a girl.

In the emergency room of the hospital, a doctor screamed at her through the soft fog that kept her safe, "What happened?"

"I had a baby. It died."

"Did you have an abortion?"

Miriam remembered. If she told anyone that she had had an abortion, she would go to jail.

"No."

"She's lying. Look, Miss," the voice screamed, "Did you have an abortion?" The voice came shrilling at her like a vulture diving in upon still and rotting flesh, like a bomb.

"No. It happened by accident." She wondered if they had heard her. She could barely hear her own voice.

"Listen, you stupid idiot, you'll die if you don't tell us the truth. We have to know what to do. I know you had an abortion. Nothing is going to happen to you. I promise. Just tell me what you used. A knitting needle? What?"

"An injection. It was an injection."

"Pack her and take her upstairs."

As packing was shoved into her vaginal canal to arrest the bleeding, another doctor came over to her and pushed her damp hair out of her eyes, not so that she would be more comfortable but so that he could see her face more clearly. "Young. Cute. Think she's going to make it?"

The first doctor with the screaming vulture voice looked into the face white and soft as clouds. People were surrounding her, hooking tubes into her arms, cutting away her nightclothes. He looked into her open empty eyes. She wanted to turn her glance away, but her eyes remained open and staring at the huge frowning face. "No. She's as good as dead."

Miriam spent six days in a city hospital. The room she was in was called semi-private, and housed ten women, including herself: five Black, three Hispanic, one Jewish, one Irish. Nine of the ten had had illegal abortions, so bungled that they were flat on their backs in bed with tubes connecting to life. One woman, from the Dominican Republic, thirty years old, the mother of eight children, was going to die. Her face was the same green as the dingy walls of the corridors leading to the room. She had tubes everywhere, in her nose, down her mouth, trailing from under her coarse white hospital robe, connecting to her urethra. A distraught man came often to visit her. At first Miriam thought the man was her son. The woman looked at least fifty, the man a weight-lifting twenty-five. The woman, Ana, could not speak English. The first day Miriam was there was the eleventh day that Ana was there. For the fourth time since she had been admitted, Ana began to hemorrhage from the nose. She leaned forward in bed, her toes sticking up from under her soiled wool blanket like the toes of a child, while blood poured from her mouth and nose into her lap. Two nurses and two aides came running into the room after the women in the room screamed and yelled for help for several minutes. Ana's roommates, helplessly pinned to their beds by their tubes hooked up to glucose feeders, by their own pain and weakness, could not help her. They desperately wanted to save her. Now the nurses were yelling at Ana in English, "Keep your head back, keep your head back." Ana began to collapse into her own lap. One of the nurses grabbed her by the hair and yanked her head back, screaming even more loudly, "Keep your head back, stupid! What's the matter, you don't even speak English?" The bleeding stopped.

Gynecological section of a city hospital. The over-crowded semi-private room, with its glass walls that were never curtained, not even when examinations were taking place, not even when there were strangers on the floor, electricians making repairs, visitors, was like a goldfish bowl. Nine women were critically ill with botched abortions, and the tenth woman had delivered a baby in the city hospital and had been sent home with a raging infection, to be readmitted close to death to the same hospital, sick with childbed fever. City hospital. New York City. Childbed fever. 1960.

Every woman wore a hospital-supplied white gown. Every woman had at least one tube needled into her body, at the arm, the ankle, or a tube shoved down the nose. Every woman in that room was learning her lesson, that she had done wrong and she must be punished. The hospital was going to teach the women that.

Sanitary conditions of a gynecological section of a city hospital. Cockroaches were visible in daylight. The floors were filthy. Ten women lay in a room, all bleeding from between their legs, a constant running flow of blood from wounds within, from violated wombs. There was a chronic shortage of sanitary napkins. At seven in the morning a nurse's aide brought to each woman a small basin of cold water. No soap, no washcloth, no cup for tooth-brushing, just a small basin of cold water. And the women who lay in the beds with old dried blood stiff and scratchy upon their smeared thighs splashed cold water upon their faces and dipped their hands. In the six days that Miriam lay in her bed she never had her sheets or gown changed.

The doctors told Miriam's parents what was wrong with her. Her father came to her room and stood at the foot of the bed, his face ashen, his mouth twisted down at the corners, his eyes dead. She looked up at him from the pillow where her black hair lay strewn in tangles, her face small and cramped and whiter than the bed linen. He looked down at her and said, "How could you do such a thing? How could you? Why did you do this to us?" Miriam turned her face away from his grief and his blame, and waited for the moment to fade and the next moment to begin. This would soon be over just as the spreading flash of pain in Mrs. Sanchez's narrow room was soon over. It was only a matter of moments, of time.

After a transfusion and with continuing intravenous feeding, Miriam was deemed strong enough to be moved to an examining room. She was wheeled on a stretcher, the bottled glucose swinging over her head, oozing into her arm. In the examining room she was hauled onto an examining table, her legs were spread by two men in white coats, and a metal speculum was shoved into her vagina. Her womb was badly infected, and the slightest touch or pressure upon it caused unbearable pain. The doctor shoved in the speculum and Miriam began to scream.

"Look, if you don't stop that screaming you'll be sorry," one of the men in white warned. Miriam couldn't stop. "Let's show her." The two men walked out of the room and closed the door. Miriam was left alone surrounded by unfamiliar grey walls, while a knife pain that was becoming familiar roared inside her. Miriam could not file the pain under "Later."

The doctors were gone for ten minutes. When they returned, with ten more men, interns in white coats, Miriam's throat felt as ripped open as her insides, and her voice was hoarse. "Please take it out," Miriam begged. No one answered her.

"Gentlemen, this is what an inflamed uterus looks like. Observe the this and that." Miriam screamed and screamed but no one was much bothered by it because her voice had faded to a dry grating shred of sound. The ten interns all took turns observing an inflamed uterus, making note of the this and that. Then all twelve men turned to leave. "Please," Miriam called, "Take it out. Please."

"In a minute."

Later the doctors came back and removed the speculum.

The second morning began with the same basin of cold water and plastic breakfast. Because some patients were on salt free diets, food was not prepared with salt. Although salt was supposed to be provided in little packets, often enough the kitchen staff did not furnish trays with salt, or the little packets of sugar, ketchup, pepper, but rather packed them up and took them home. As they took home the white meat of turkey, with its stiffly frozen aftertaste, the slices of cheese on waxed paper. Big and little packages of pre-packed food by the pound. The soft-boiled eggs were cold. The milk for the cereal was warm. And then, the visit to the examining room.

On the second day the doctor, after a prolonged examination with speculum, left the weeping young woman alone in the room, still with speculum inserted, while he went off to his desk to write up his observations. After completing his report, he removed the speculum, and then examined her digitally, inserting his finger with such jarring force and roughness that she screamed again. "Come on," he scolded, "you know it doesn't hurt. Don't be such a baby."

The third morning a nurse's aide came dashing into the room late. "Sorry, girls, I'm fifteen minutes behind schedule today, so no water this morning."

There was a sleepy silence in the room. Then Miriam protested, "Oh no. Look, we do without hot water and soap, but we can't do without any water at all. I have to wash up a little. I'm really a mess."

"You sure are a mess, girl. Don't bother me. I'm late."

"You're not leaving without getting us our water."

"Who says?" The aide left. Five minutes later two nurses and a staff doctor came running down the hall and into the room, faster than they had when Ana had spilled blood from her nose and mouth into her bloated lap.

"Who was making the big fuss in here?" the doctor asked. No one answered. The nurse's aide waddled into the room behind the doctor. She pointed at Miriam. "That's the one, the one with the big fresh mouth."

"Look, if you make a fuss and bother our staff, we'll remove you to G ward for observation. No more trouble out of you, you understand? You're lucky you're alive. Don't look for trouble here, or you'll get it. If you think you'll like G Ward better than GYN, open your mouth again." The nurses, the doctor, and the nurse's aide left. And Miriam contemplated her possible transfer to G Ward, for suspected psychotics, as punishment for asking for cold water to wash with in the morning.

"You know, I haven't seen that many doctors and nurses together on this floor in all the time I've been here," a woman slowly said. "You must be really sick." All the women laughed.

"Sick and tired," Miriam answered. The women laughed again. "But listen, don't you mind not getting water this morning?"

"A few days more and we'll be home again. Why make trouble. They ain't gonna give us nothing. Why get yourself all upset?"

In the examining room later that morning ten more interns got a chance to view a badly infected uterus. Miriam did not think of wondering why her uterus was badly infected, or whether it was showing signs of clearing up.

The fourth day a woman intern examined Miriam. She was very short, Asian, with a round face, short wavy hair, and a prematurely puckered brow. Her voice was lightly accented, softly lilting, and her fingers were cool and light. "I know this is going to hurt you," she apologized, "but I will be as careful and as quick as I can. I'm sorry."

Quickly, carefully, delicately, she examined Miriam. It hurt, but not enough to make Miriam scream. Afterward, she smiled at the doctor. "You were really very gentle."

"I know how much it must hurt. Your womb is badly infected and must clear up. I really don't want to hurt you."

It occurred to Miriam that the men who did hurt her might really want to hurt her. She put that in the file marked "Later."

The fifth day a nurse's aide came in the early evening, after the last plastic meal of the day, and began to regulate the intravenous glucose flow dripping with monotonous rhythm into Miriam's arm. Miriam felt with some alarm that she could feel a great increase of flow, that her arm, which was stiff and sore from being strapped to a board and pierced with needles for five days, felt as if it were starting to swell.

"I think you increased the flow too much," Miriam said. "Could you please turn it down a little?"

"Don't tell me how to do my job," the aide snapped.

"I'm not. It's just that the needle is in my arm and I can feel the flow and it's too much. My arm feels all swollen."

"I know what I'm doing. Your arm's all right."

Miriam kept trying. Her arm felt as if glucose were being pumped into her, like gasoline into a car tank, overwhelming her flesh, overflowing her blood vessels, spilling into her tissues and clogging the hinges of her elbow and wrist and shoulder. "Look, the needle's in my arm and I can feel it flowing too fast."

"Well, Miss Big Mouth, I wish the needle were in your mouth instead of your arm."

Nothing to think about. Miriam was angry. "And I wish the needle was up your ass."

"You can't speak to me that way. Who do you think you are? Look where you are, everybody knows what you're here for. You can't talk to me like that. The doctor's going to hear about this."

In under five minutes, record speed, a staff doctor and two nurses came running into the room.

"You again," the doctor said. "We have quite a record on you. You're really a trouble maker, aren't you? These girls have hard enough jobs without getting any trouble from the patients. Do you want to be sent to G Ward?"

Miriam's breath began to stutter, hard dry gasps that sounded like machinery breaking down. She was trying not to cry. "Well, big mouth, do you? You're not too big mouthed now, are you? Think you can curse out a nurse's aide, right? Got a mouth on you like a sewer. We know what kind of girl you are, we know why you're here. Well, let's hear you curse out a doctor. Or don't you want to be sent to G Ward?"

The women in the room breathed in a conspiratorial unison,

listening to the doctor. The two nurses and the aide stood at the door like back-up troops.

"We don't need any trouble-makers down here. One more word out of you, and off you go." The doctor wheeled on his heel in best military form, and left. The aide flounced off down the hall after him, grinning. One of the nurses walked over to Miriam's bed, and bent over Miriam's arm, which was swollen and spongy with the excess fluid from the too rapid flow. She adjusted the mechanism back to a slower rate. "The swelling will subside. Don't worry about it." Her voice, though impersonal, had an undertone of feeling to it, possibly fear. She did not look at Miriam's face.

Miriam was scheduled for a routine dilation and curettage on her sixth day in the hospital, to be performed just prior to discharge. The scheduled operation never took place. Instead, the needle was removed from her arm and she was allowed to walk around. She went straight to the toilet and rinsed away, with warm water and wadded up toilet paper and soap, the dried and stinking blood that covered her thighs, vagina, belly.

Dilation and curettage. Miriam no longer had to worry about it. She happily filed it under "Past". She had had a secret dread of the operation, of the anesthesia, the entire process of spreading her legs open once again to the unknown. The result of spreading her legs to the unknown was always, obviously, pain.

Dilation and curettage. It was routinely performed to rid the uterus of any matter remaining from a possibly incomplete and therefore unclean abortion. Scraps of placenta, coagulated blood, were removed. The staff called it a D and C. The patients called it a scraping. The word "scraping" made Miriam feel as if the marrow in her bones was shriveling. At the thought of the word she could feel a raw sensation in her lower belly, as if her womb were being scraped with a steel file, or a carding comb, or the edge of an index card. When the operation was cancelled, Miriam felt only relief. She didn't ask whether or not her infected uterus had returned to normal, or whether there was any sign of infection in her body, or what was being left behind in her womb. She was afraid of dying, now that she had survived.

On the seventh day Miriam was discharged from the hospital

as fully cured. The doctor who made the routine rounds stopped by her bed and said, brusquely, "No coito por seis semanas." Miriam didn't go straight home. Her parents came to pick her up, and brought her to the family doctor's office. He examined her, gave her a blood test, and told her to go home and rest. Later that evening he telephoned to say that Miriam must remain in bed with absolutely no exertion for a full two weeks. She was not even to get up for meals, but was to have food brought to her on a tray. Preferably she was not even to get up to go to the toilet but was to use a bed pan, which Miriam refused. The bed rest was absolutely necessary, for she had a raging infection of the uterus, and if it didn't show signs of abatement she was to undergo a hysterectomy. Miriam sighed, closed her eyes, and stayed in bed for two weeks, taking antibiotics, having regular blood tests, and filing it all under "Later". She read *Crime and Punishment* by Dostoevsky, a gift from Rob, to take her mind off her troubles.

The infection responded to treatment. She did not need to undergo a hysterectomy. After two weeks she was permitted to take up again a life that might best be described, like certain children, as slow-normal.

She refused to see Barry again. She planned to return the rest of the money, the extra one hundred and fifty dollars, but a girlfriend came to her in mute terror, pregnant, and Miriam lent her the money to build an abortion fund. The friend raised a thousand dollars and went to the Virgin Islands. She said it was the best vacation of her life, and she never paid back the money. Therefore Barry's house plan had the privilege of paying for two abortions.

Rob came often to see Miriam. After three weeks he began to pressure her to make love. They had not been lovers for almost a year.

"I can't. The doctor said six weeks."

"But you're all right. Come on, baby."

So she did. He was very careful, and didn't put it in all the way, and of course he wore a rubber. She didn't feel much. Any pleasure she might be able to feel was put in the file marked "Later".

When he tried to caress her with his hands, with his mouth,

to kindle pleasure in her, she drew back, terrified. Vulva, hands, speculum, touch, pain. Don't touch. You can put it in, but don't touch. Hands hurt. Men's hands, doctors' hands, hurt, hurt, hurt. Later she would feel what was happening. Later.

Rob slipped into memory. Like water, through laxly laced fingers. Another memory, and another. He drifted back to his cool, full-breasted blonde women, and Miriam married someone.

In 1962, Miriam's first living baby was born. In 1964, another. In 1966, another. She did so have a uterus. She could too have real live babies.

"Come on, baby. Let me put it in. I'll be careful. Let me put it in. Just a little."

I have told Miriam's story as truthfully as I have been able. I believe that this story is true. I have told this truth as the enduring private holocaust of woman's flesh, the flaming consumption of lives, the purgatory sealed into the meat and hollows of body so that people will know and remember. That is my commitment to story.

Chapter Two
LAZARUS

You can't name a child Lazarus! That's no name for a child!"

"It's his name. It has to be his name. He is Lazarus."

"All the other kids will tease him. No one gets named Lazarus! They'll call him Lazy for short. Lazy Lazarus. Think about it!"

"I'm thinking about it! I'm thinking about everything! He's alive! He's a living miracle! And besides, it's none of your business! He's my child, not yours, and his name is Lazarus!"

I thought about it.

"Ain't nobody's business but my own."

I never was supposed to have a baby. I wasn't a pretty girl. I wasn't ugly, but I was plain. People would tell me to exercise, or eat better, to get some color in my cheeks. I was sallow, they told me, I was pale. I was wan. They didn't say I was wan – wan isn't exactly a big word, it doesn't have a lot of syllables. Still, they didn't know the word. But I did. My name is Wanda, and when I looked up my name to see what it means, I found the word "wan" first. Do you know what "etymology" means? It means where a word comes from. "Wan" is weird. It comes from the Old English. Old English is a Germanic language, but there isn't any other Germanic language that has the word "wan". It is straight up English, Old English, and it is weird because it means pale, pasty, ashen, but it also means dark, leaden, grey. And all of that is all of me. Outside I am pale, pasty, ashen, inside I am dark, leaden, grey. One dictionary says the word might be related to the word "wane". Am I on the wane? Am I going out before I let my little light shine? If I am on the wane, then once upon a time I must have had at least a little glow, a little spark, a hint of flame.

Old English. My father used to wear Old English cologne. My mother used to use Old English furniture polish. So what? We still weren't English. We were hardly American even. We were common. That's what people said about us. We were common. Well, common should be good. It means shared, doesn't it? But no one shared anything with us. We were different, and still, we were common. People said common. They meant low. But we weren't low. My father was proud of his appearance, and got his nails manicured when most men we knew didn't, and he wore cologne, and he dressed natty. And my mother cleaned the house all the time, and used furniture polish, and waxed the floors.

Wanda. My mother was part Polish, and part Ukrainian. Wanda is a Polish name. it has something to do with an old Polish tribe, the Wends. Is being Polish low? You heard all the Polish jokes, right? We're supposed to be stupid. But I know how to look up words in the dictionary, and I know what definition, and etymology, and derivation, and synonym, and antonym, mean, and I know what root words are. My mother wasn't stupid, and her Polish mother wasn't stupid, and I'm not as stupid as all the kids and a lot of the teachers thought I was.

My father was other stuff. Irish and Dutch and what he called Canuck, but what he meant was French Canadian and some kind of Canadian Indian, MicMac. I once told some kids I was part MicMac, and since my last name is Irish, they knew I was at least part Irish, so they started to sing, "MicMac, Paddy whack, give the dog a bone, stupid Wanda should go home".

There's a song with the words, "I'm a wanderer. I go round and round and round and round". Wanderer is a word derived from Old German. From wend, meaning turn, like in wend your way. There's another song that comes from the Bible, "Turn, turn, turn, for every season, turn, turn, turn". Were the Polish Wends wanderers? Do they go round and round and round and round, do they turn, turn, turn, turn? If they didn't, I do.

"We go round in circles, we go round like a bird up in the sky." That's another line from the wanderer song. And then there's a real American folk song. American, from the common people. The song is called "The Little Leather-Winged Bat", and it has a verse that says, "Hi, said the little birds going round, we fly in circles above the ground, the circles get smaller every year, and by and by, we disappear".

People want me to disappear. They want the real me to disappear, and a made-up Wanda, a Wanda they want me to be, to take my place. They say I can't name my baby Lazarus. But my baby's name was Lazarus before he was born, before he was made in my body, before I was born. He was meant to be Lazarus.

Do you know what Lazarus means? It's from the Christian Bible, but the name is Hebrew, "El Azar", "God helps". And my baby is Lazarus because he is helping me. We are going to love each other. That helps.

There's another name that means God helps, and it is the same name as Lazarus, but the name is Eleazar. Anytime you see a Hebrew word with "el" in it, the "el" means God. And I guess "azar" always means helps. So Eleazar is the real Hebrew name, and Lazarus is a way to say Eleazar, but it is more Greek or Latin than Hebrew. That's confusing to me. Does that mean that Greeks and Latins said Lazarus, but Jews said Eleazar? I'm not Jewish, but I'm not a Greek or a Latin either.

I learned about the two men named Lazarus in the Christian Bible, and their stories are interesting. In one story a man named Lazarus died, and Jesus raised him from the dead. Jesus brought him back to life. And in another story Lazarus was a very poor man, and he begged for bread at the rich man's gate, and the rich man said no.

Well, in that second story, that is what is happening with my son Lazarus. I told you I wasn't ever supposed to have a baby. I wasn't pretty. And people said my family was common. The kids in school didn't like me. I wanted to like them, but how do you like somebody who doesn't like you? So I didn't have any friends. And then, in high school, they liked me even less than they liked me before. They got meaner. One day as I was going up the steps to the door to go to school, I passed a bunch of boys, and one boy said to the others, "The only way I would fuck her is if I put a flag over her face and fucked her for Old Glory". And everybody laughed. Even some girls who were standing nearby laughed. Girls are not supposed to laugh at stuff like that. But they laughed. They weren't laughing at the fucking part. They were laughing at me.

After that, every time we said the Pledge of Allegiance in the morning, in the auditorium during General Assembly before we went to our home rooms, when I put my hand over my heart, all the kids around me began to laugh.

But I still went to school. I liked learning stuff. I liked the classes, and the books. None of the teachers liked me particularly, but they didn't hate me, and they didn't make fun of me. Some even gave me good marks on my test papers, and on my essays in English and history, and some of them even recommended books I would like.

So I didn't go out on dates. I didn't want to. Who would want to go out on a date with a boy who was mean and who would laugh at you? Not me. There were no boys who were nice to me, so I didn't want to go out on dates with them. And I knew I would never meet a movie star or a rock star or any other cute guy I saw on television or in the movies or heard on the radio.

Some teachers said I should go to college. But I was afraid of college. So after I finished high school I got a job. It was an okay job, nothing exciting, but nothing too hard. Just easy enough.

Long story short. There was a grown-up man where I worked, who worked with me. He wasn't so many years older than me. He wasn't a "man man", I mean a too old man. He wasn't a kid either, he wasn't a teenager like me, or even 21 or 22. He was 27, nine years older than me. And we went out on a few dates together. I didn't tell my parents, though. I met him downtown.

Oh, so I got pregnant. What did you think would happen? Of course I got pregnant. It was inevitable. See, that's not a very big word. It's got five syllables, but everyone knows what it means. Oh. I bet you're wondering, what did I think would happen? I didn't know I should think about what would happen. No one ever gave me any advice about getting pregnant. My parents knew I didn't go out on dates, they knew I wasn't pretty. And I didn't have any girls to be friends with who would tell me about this either. Oh. Yes, I took the high school hygiene class. That's what they called the sex education class – the hygiene class. And they told us not to have sex before we were ready for responsibility, and the best way to be ready for responsibility was to be married. And they told us not to get pregnant unless we had enough money because having a baby was very expensive. And other stuff. They told us other stuff too.

But I didn't really pay attention, because I wasn't going to have sex or even kiss anyone. I was going to read the dictionary sometimes, and a bunch of other books. Not story books. Not novels. Books about things, about how things worked, or about geology. I liked reading about how the earth was formed, and how the earth worked. And about rocks. Mostly about rocks. Sedimentary, metamorphic, igneous rocks. And I liked learning what those words meant. I liked knowing the roots of those rock words, the etymology. I think it would be great if a famous rock star sang songs about real rocks.

Here's a rock song I made up:

Igneous rock rocks, it once was hot, and now it's chill,
It comes from volcanoes, from deep in the earth,
There's great upheaval, and the volcano gives birth
to magma, then boiling lava, look out, it can kill,
but soon it gets real cool, and forms sleek rock
pitch black sometimes, so don't anybody mock
rock, volcanic rock, igneous rock!
Sedimentary rock accumulates, it takes every kind
of big rocks, little rocks, joining with each other,
a piece here, a piece there, as if some master mind
said, become a family, big sister and little brother.
Metamorphic rock changes, it's the real superhero,
When you put on the pressure on the other kinds of rock,
the rock survives, it never dies, it never becomes a zero.
So, heat and weight are pressure, but the rock's no laughing stock,
Rock on, metamorphic, eternally morphing, tough as rock, rock!

Well, those are the lyrics. The melody and the musical arrangement, I can't do that. Maybe someone will some day. Maybe when Lazarus grows up he will be a musician and turn all my lyrics into real songs. Maybe he'll play guitar and sing. I'll buy him a guitar, and a little keyboard, and find a music teacher who doesn't charge too much, who'll teach him to play. Or maybe when I have some money I'll buy a guitar and keyboard for me, now, and a book that can teach me how to play, and maybe I can even learn to make up the melody too.

Oh. So, the 27-year-old man said he didn't want a baby, and he would pay for an abortion. I thought about it, but I wanted a baby. So I said no. He said he couldn't marry me. I don't know what "couldn't" meant. I asked why he couldn't, and he said it just wouldn't be right, we couldn't, we shouldn't. And then, a few days later, he didn't work where I worked any more, and when I went to the little place where he rented a room, where we had sex, he didn't live there any more either. He was just gone.

I wasn't in love with him anyway. I just liked having him for a boyfriend. My first boyfriend ever. I felt like a regular girl, having a boyfriend. And an older boyfriend. It meant I was sophisticated, that I was interesting, if a 27-year-old man liked to go out with me and talk to me. And he was pretty interesting too. He had lived all sorts of places, all over America. He said he grew up an Army brat, that his father was in the military – I never heard anybody say "in the military" before, it meant his father was a professional army man – and his father was sent to army bases all over the country. So this boyfriend – his name is Walter – lived everywhere, and he was really funny. He could do regional accents – regional means from a region, from a part of the country. He could do Southern accents, and cowboy accents, and California girl accents, and upper class New England Boston accents, and corn belt accents. That's what he called it—corn belt. He meant the part of the country in the Midwest where corn grows, where there are big corn farms – and big pig farms too. And the funniest accent he did was a Brooklyn accent. You could die laughing listening to him talk like people from Brooklyn. He also explained that there were all different kinds of Southern accents. My favorite one was the one from New Orleans. N'awlins, he said.

Where am I from? I don't want to say. Well, okay. My family lived outside of Pittsburgh.

So I decided to have my baby, because I knew I could love my baby, and my baby could love me. And then I had to go on bed rest or I might have a miscarriage. I couldn't work, I couldn't live with my parents any more, I went on welfare and found a woman's shelter to live in. And I didn't have a miscarriage. But my baby came early. Was way underweight. They told me he might not live. But he lived. And I said I was going to name him Lazarus, because I was going to pull him back from the dead with my heart and my mind. I was going to wish him to be alive.

And now he's alive and he weighs enough and he lives with me and his name is Lazarus, and we don't have any money, we're on the welfare. I went down to the welfare office, which I made believe was the house of the rich man named Dives, from the Bible, the one who turned Lazarus from the Bible, the poor beggar, away without any bread. And I decided I was going to help Dives become a good man, who wouldn't turn us away.

And Dives the welfare worker became a good man, and didn't turn us away. Now I live in a nice little room. I have my own mattress. I don't have a bed frame, the mattress is on the floor, but I keep the floor very clean. It's a wood floor, and I rinse it with a damp mop, and wax it. Wax is expensive, of course, but I just use a little bit, a little bit can go a long way, and I make it last. A waxed floor is easier to sweep. I learned that from my mother. I have a mattress, and some throw pillows I found at the thrift store. So the throw pillows make it look like a fancy divan from the Arabian nights, a place to lounge. A divan is a word that means a place to lie down and lie around, like a sofa, but without arms or anything. The word is from the Persian. People in Turkey and Persia and other places like that would lie around on divans. Very fancy. And now I can too.

Divan and Dives have nothing to do with each other.

And Lazarus has a crib. When he gets too old for the crib, I'll put the crib mattress on the floor, so he won't bump into the sides of the crib, so the sides won't be too tight.

And I have a tiny little table to eat off—it's a card table, and I have three chairs to go with it. And some pots and pans, and a few dishes, and some tableware, forks and spoons and knives and stuff, and two cups, and two glasses, all from the Good Will store.

I already had clothing. And the welfare helped me get clothing for my baby too, and baby blankets and stuff.

So nobody can tell me what to name my baby. Lazarus and I keep coming back from the dead, and we can find places where the rich man will give us bread.

But most of all, I am Wanda, and I am not wandering, I am not going around in circles, I am not stupid, no one is the boss of me, and I am here, and I won't disappear.

"This little light of mine, I'm gonna let it shine..."

Chapter Three
DANILA

I don't know what to do next. The future already happened.

There's nothing to do. Everything already happened, everything exists far into the future. I try to imagine possibility, but nothing is possible—because the future already happened.

I learned about time and space somewhere – maybe in my high school physics class. Maybe on a television science show, or in a television show set in the future, or maybe on the internet. But I learned that time is eternal, that past, present, and future are a constant, that time is not linear, time just is, and the future happened.

So there's nothing to do. I don't do nothing, though. I do something anyway.

Yesterday a person asked me, "What is your name?" I wanted to ask the person, "What do you mean by your, what do you mean by name, what do you mean by your name", but I know that persons get confused when I ask those kinds of questions, so I answered the person with a name that persons have told me is my name. I said, "My name is Danila".

I think sometimes when persons ask "What is your name?" they expect you to answer, and then ask, "What is your name?" Should I have asked? I didn't. And then the person said, "My name is Dr. Wiggins". Then the Dr. Wiggins person said, "Would you like to call me Dr. Wiggins? My first name is Ernest. You can call me Ernest. Would you like to call me Ernest? Or Dr. Wiggins?"

That's a whole heap of questions. Dr. Ernest Wiggins person likes to ask a whole heap of questions at once.

"Dr. Ernest Wiggins person, you ask a whole heap of questions at once. Which one would you like me to answer first?"

Ay de mi. Oy vey. Goodness gracious. He looked confused, and then he laughed a little bit, and then he said, "Whichever question you would like to answer."

I said, "I will call you Dr. Ernest Wiggins person until I figure out what to call you", and that's what I did.

Most of the time I just call him “Person”. That’s what I call most persons. But if there are a number of persons around, they can’t usually tell from my vocal intonation which person I mean when I say “Person”, so I call them a name they respond to. I call Dr. Ernest Wiggins person “Doc”, or “Ernie”. He calls me “Danila” or “Dani”.

Names locate us, names give us a time/space locus. “My name is Danila” is my time/space locus, so persons can locate not just me, but themselves. Each of us is a time/space locus whose center is everywhere and whose circumference is nowhere, because each of us is an emanation of the Divine, and the Divine is that whose center is everywhere and whose circumference is nowhere. Someone told me that a time/space locus person named Alain de Lille, who wandered around time/space in what persons call the 12th century CE, said that, and someone told me that a time/space locus person named Blaise Pascal, who wandered around time/space in what persons call the 17th century CE, also said that.

I like this: “It may be that universal history is the history of the different intonations given a handful of metaphors”, which time/space locus person Jorge Luis Borges said when he wrote about the metaphor of the infinite sphere, which is a metaphor for the metaphor of the Divine. I like to intone, and listen to intonations. Intonations are variants of pitch, of the human voice or any other sound-creating paraphernalia, a musical instrument or the wind in the trees or the incoming ocean tide or the cry of beast or fowl. I will take an image, a metaphor, and intone it, and sing the metaphor song to persons, or to the wind, or the ocean, or beasts or fowl.

Time/space locus person William Butler Yeats said, “And when I pay attention I must out and walk among the dogs and horses that understand my talk. O what of that, O what of that, what is there left to say?”

Some time/locus persons understand the language of the birds, and the birds understand the language of those time/locus persons, just like dogs and horses do. I talk to birds, horses, dogs, poets in their poem words, and to the internet, and to myself.

Wiggins is a funny name. What to say to Wiggins: Do you live in a wigwam? Do you wear a toupee? Can you wiggle your ears?

Do you sing the "Wiggle" along with Jason DeRulo, and dance the Wiggle Dance? Wiggle Dance is not the same as Waggle Dance. Bee persons dance the Waggle Dance. Look, bee persons say, this way is pollen, here pollen lies, this is where the honey of the future is, and the future already happened, so this pollen is honey. The Wiggle Dance is about a honey pot. That's different.

What else to say to Wiggins: Did you wig out? Are you Uncle Wiggily, and do you come from Connecticut, and are you a fictional character created by J.D. Salinger, and if you are, how did you escape from the pages of the novel and become a doctor? Do you think that I am wigged out, and is that why you came to see me?

Or, Dr. Wiggins, did you escape from the pages of "The Importance of Being Ernest", by Oscar Wilde? Do you wig out and go wild, earnestly? Can a person be earnestly wild? Or wildly earnest? Dr. E.W. wants to know everything about a person he says I should call "me", or "I", a "Danila" person. "Tell me about yourself, Danila...."

"Me". Tell "me" about "yourself". Dr. E.W. person means tell himself about me, and me is I, and I is Danila, so here goes.

Age: Depends where in time/space locus, where in the divine sphere whose center is everywhere and whose circumference is nowhere, you catch me.

Dr. E. W. says "Now", so I say, "Seventeen".

Family: Huh?

Family: Oh. Family. Yes. I was born. I am still born. But I wasn't stillborn. I also am still unborn. What was my face before I was born? What does "before" mean?

Family: Oh. Family. Yes. Organic, animal, mammal, hominid, human, mother, father, ancestors, siblings, generations past, generations future....

Family: Oh. Family. Her time/space locus person name is Mommy. His time/space locus person name is Dad. He calls her Della, and she calls him Mel, and sometimes they call each other other words. My time/space locus persons brothers are Mr. Darcy and Mr. Toad, and they are 23 years old and 20 years old, and my time/space locus person sister is Alice in Wonderland, and she is

14, and my imaginary companion's name is Danila, and she is me.

Mommy owns a bakery, and Dad doesn't. He stays home and drinks alcohol more than Mommy likes him to, but I don't care, because he never seems drunk, he just seems lonely, and he has to stay lonely, because no one wants to talk to him, because he is a dark shadow, he is a dark cloud, he is too vague and not well drawn, and so we ignore him. He is lonely, and he ignores everyone anyway.

Mommy brings home bread and pastries.

I don't live there any more. I live here with you, Dr. E.W. Now. You like "Now". I also live in that Mommy and Dad house too, and I live somewhere in the future, away from them and away from you. I live far in the future, which already happened, and if I tell you about it, you think I am imagining, or making things up, but I know about time and space and I am there already.

I had a teacher in high school physics who liked the name Ms. Stanton, and we time/space locus persons she called "students" called her Ms. Stanton. I explained to her about time is all the time, all time happened and is happening forever, and she said I was an eternalist, that I believe in a block universe. So I told her I always enjoyed playing with blocks when I was a little girl, and I was building time castles with time, I was building an Eternal City.

Change is an illusion. Dr. E.W. wants me to change, to get better. He worries about whether I am better or worse. But change is an illusion. I tell him to stop trying to nickel and dime me with his picture of the universe, his small change version of reality, I like my version, and I'm not trying to nickel and dime change him, so he should leave me alone.

I used to have a pet, a kitty cat, named Shro. Ms. Stanton person was trying to understand quantum entanglement, but she was having a hard time explaining it to us, the "student" persons in her class. I told her my kitty cat was a dual-system kitty cat, that once each system interacted with each other, but now were separate, so that Shro was sometimes alive and sometimes dead. She didn't understand what I was saying. I told her my kitty cat could have been locked in a steel cage by the creator of all cats, Shrödinger, but I knew how to unlock the steel cage and let Shro out. Only in the steel cage was my kitty cat alive and dead, and that was so entangled it couldn't be unknotted. Ms. Stanton person thought I was going to strangle my kitty cat, or kill it because I thought I could bring it back to life, and she reported me to a guidance counselor person at the high school, and the guidance counselor person reported me to Mommy and Dad, and now I live in the here and now with Dr. E.W. person, but not really, because I live in eternity, with all reality, among all the eternalists, and I am just dropping in at this space/time locus point.

I never hurt my kitty cat. When Mommy and Dad checked on Shro, Shro was curled up on a window seat in my bedroom, reading my physics textbook, which was lying open where I left it, and Shro was healthy and breathing. They didn't know how to check on Shro seven years later than that moment, and maybe Shro was alive seven years later also, but they don't know, because they think seven years later hasn't happened yet.

I keep happening, though.

Dr. E.W. person asked me if I fantasized about strangling my kitty cat, and I asked Dr. E.W. person if he fantasized about me killing my kitty cat, and, if he did, what did that mean to him, and he laughed a little.

I think that should be his soul name, his bush name – Dr. Laugh-a-Little.

Is there a difference between fantasy and thinking?

I think, therefore I was... and am... and will be... eternally...

Chapter Four
READER, I MARRIED HIM

Reader, I married him. Don't skip ahead to the end.

Oh. But... that's not the end. It might be a frightful beginning, it might be in medias res, but that's not the end.

Don't skip ahead to the end. The story doesn't end with Reader, I murdered him. Coulda woulda shoulda, but didn't.

What matters now, is....

Anyway, remember the Shirelles singing, "I met him on a Sunday...", 1958? And the chorus was something like, "Doo ron ron ron, de doo ron ron"? Or maybe it was the Crystals, singing, "Da doo ron ron ron, well, I met him on a Monday, and his name was Bill, and my heart stood still....", 1963? Well, his name was Ron. Da doo ron ron ron, da doo ron ron, either way. Do Wrong Ron.

What did he do right? Well, he totally rocked his good genes, and his good jeans. Looked like Elvis Presley, kinda, and wore good jeans right. Did he sing like Elvis Presley? No. Did he sing? No. Did he swivel his hips like Elvis Presley? No. Did he swivel his hips when he danced? Yes. But who didn't? Doo ron ron ron, da doo ron ron.

High school graduate. Okay, he wasn't a high school drop-out, but so what? He wasn't much of anything anyway. College? Community college drop-out. Okay, lots of guys don't go to college, but they're decent guys, and some are actually smart, and some of those are actually not only smart, they're book smart too, even if they didn't go to college. They work, and they read.

I read. You might not know from the way I talk, but I read a lot, and, guess what, I went to college. All the way. B.A. Not just community college, four-year college, all the way. I wanted to teach. And I learned how to be a teacher. Guess what. I'm a teacher. I teach art in a public school in a school district that still has a budget for art education and an art teacher, and I teach art in a middle school, and, well, guess what, I'm good at it, and the kids love my classes. I have lots and lots and lots of art supplies, some of which I actually buy myself, because even if I don't have a school budget for everything, I have my own money for whatever

I want, and I don't want much except art supplies for myself, and for the classes. I also imagine all sorts of wonderful projects to do with kids, and they love what I dream up for them, because my projects teach them to look, to keep looking, and to imagine, and to imagine beyond imagining, and to find themselves in the middle of the art project, just being themselves in the middle of all the stuff that artists do.

Once upon a time an English teacher in high school taught us about Zen koans – two words no one in the class, except the teacher, knew, and, once she taught us about Zen koans, we all knew about Zen, and about koans, and about imagining what a Zen koan means. If you don't know about Zen koans, you can look it up on the internet. Besides which, everyone knows about Zen nowadays, even if they don't know about koans. When you read a magazine and you see the beautiful expensive apartments and houses of very rich people, celebrities or business people, a lot of the rooms, and gardens, are described as being very Zen. You get the impression that if you have money, you can get Zen. Well, like the Beatles said, money can't buy you love, and, like I say, money can't buy you Zen. Zen isn't an apartment or a house or a meditation room or a garden.

Zen. Well, Zen is a way of knowing from being within yourself and paying attention. That's all. Sometimes a good Zen teacher can help you discover how to be within yourself and how to pay attention, but, even then, the Zen teacher can't teach you Zen. Only you can. Or at least, that's what my high school English teacher said, and, you know what, later, when I read more about Zen, I found out she knew something about Zen, she was right.

Koan. No one really explains koan right. Koan is a challenge. It can be a story, or a question, or a statement. One way to think about it is to see it as a challenge to think. But not to think the way we mean when we say think. Say a koan is a problem to solve, and we solve problems by thinking them through. Like math problems. Step by step. Or a way of understanding history.

For instance, a high school history teacher may ask, what were the causes of the American Civil War? And you read a lot about the times then, what was going on then, and find out that black people were slaves, and didn't have any freedom because they were black, and white people in the South used the black people as slaves so they could make money growing and selling cotton, and white people in the Caribbean, which is not the United States, but is near it, used black people as slaves so they could make money growing sugar cane and selling sugar and molasses and that kind of sugar stuff. There were no white slaves at that time in history. So some free white people thought keeping people as slaves was not fair, was not right, was totally wrong, that all people should be free. And equal.

So then, you read all this stuff about then, and you wonder. Was the American Civil War about whether owning slaves was wrong? Was it about black people and white people being the same, that all that stuff about skin color or hair texture didn't matter? Was it about wanting to keep the money from selling cotton and sugar and that kind of stuff, because you made more money if you didn't have to pay people to work in the cotton fields or the sugar cane fields? Was it about states' rights, meaning that states could do what the state governments said, not what the federal government said? Or other stuff? That's a big problem to think about and answer—what caused the American Civil War? And, imagine, thinking about all those questions before that war began. Those were big big problems to solve. Should there be slaves? Are white people and black people the same or different, and if they are different, what about that matters?

Well, thinking about that kind of problem is not the same thing as—what—thinking about?—I don't know if that's the right way to say it, but I'll say it for now, so I can say something—thinking about a Zen koan.

A Zen koan is a challenge. So—do we think about it? Or consider it? Or just let it sink in and be with it? I don't know how to explain it. I know what I mean, but I can't say it right.

Anyway, my favorite Zen koan is a very famous one, one that a lot of people know, one that a lot of people probably say is their favorite one. Are we supposed to have a favorite Zen koan? Is having a favorite wrong Zen, not Zen? I don't know. And I don't know how to say what I mean about all this. But I do know that I love this Zen koan. So, the Zen koan is:

"What was your face before you were born?"

So, about my art class. I say to my students that they can use any materials they find in the class, regular art supplies like paint and chalk and pastels and crayons and magic markers and brushes and pencils and paper, plain paper and colored paper, heavy paper and regular paper, clay and glue and scissors and glitter and little pieces of ribbon. And they can use other stuff I bring in, like twigs and acorns and little stones and gravel and broken up small pieces of brick and dried flowers and dry pasta pieces, macaroni and stuff that you buy in a box, and some dried beans, stuff like that.

And I say to them, "What was your face before you were born?", and ask them to show me with their art supplies.

Some of them just plain old love it—they grab stuff and start making images, start putting stuff together, finding what they see inside themselves as their face before they were born. Some of them just kind of stand still, staring out, and then some of those say, "I don't understand. What do you mean?" And I say, "I don't understand either. So don't try to understand. Just wonder. Wonder with your hands, and your art supplies". And, you know what? They understand that. They understand wondering. If you don't understand, wonder. Wonder with your hands. And they do.

So I'm a good art teacher. Because I wonder with my hands and art supplies, and anything I can hold I can use as an art supply. If I wonder, then just by wondering, I can invite other people to wonder too.

It took me a long time to become an art teacher. Do Wrong Ron and I went out on dates, and we got intimate—you know what I mean, right?—and I got pregnant, and Do Wrong Ron said he wanted to do the right thing, and, Reader, he married me.

So I graduated from high school, looking real chubby, but the graduation gown covered up my being chubby, and I wore a loose graduation dress too, which was weird, but I was used to being weird, because I was an artist even then, I was an artist ever since I was a little kid, and four months later, I had a baby, and we named her Roxanne, which was Ron's favorite girl's name, and I thought it was a really really pretty name too.

But Ron never held a job for very long. And he smoked a lot of weed. I told him he couldn't smoke in the house because it wasn't good for the baby, and, although he never really listened to me, he listened to me about this, because he said he really really loved Roxie. But we never had any money, I couldn't buy any clothes for myself or for Roxie, and I always had baby food for her, but not always enough food for Ron and me, and he would yell at me for not knowing how to budget and for wasting the household money. I made rice and beans, and beans and rice, and pasta and beans, and beans and pasta, and peanut butter and jelly sandwiches, and peanut butter sandwiches, and jelly sandwiches, and cornflakes and milk, and Rice Krispies and milk, and Spam sandwiches, and sometimes tuna salad. And I always bought apples and bananas.

One day Ron said he was tired of living with me and watching me waste his hard earned money, and he left. I thought since he said he really really really loved Roxie, he would come and visit and take her out. She was four years old, and she was easy to go places with. He could take her to the playground, or the public library, they were free. But he didn't. He was gone. Solid gone.

So I took her to the playground when the weather was okay, and to the public library, and sometimes just strange places that didn't cost anything. In those days some of the museums were free, and one wasn't too far away. It was a long walk, but we wanted to go, and so we walked. And I took her to different churches and stuff, not when they had services, because, you know, I didn't want her to learn all that "shouldn't" stuff they teach, but I wanted her to see the different kinds of beautiful architecture.

This is the way it seemed to me then: Some churches look like churches looked in Europe back in the olden times, very fancy, with high high ceilings up to the roof, and the ceilings, or roofs, were arched. They also had little alcoves you could walk into, and stained glass windows. We would walk around and look at the stained glass pictures, and the statues too. But, you know, those kind of churches, the statues and the stained glass are kind of weird. They have crosses hung on the wall, and on the crosses Jesus is being crucified, and that's pretty yucky, and when Roxie began asking questions about that, we didn't go there any more.

Later, when I went to college, I learned all about the architecture and art work in those Roman Catholic churches. I learned about Gothic architecture, and vaulted ceilings, and medieval and Renaissance art.

We also went to Protestant churches. They were very plain, very simple, with a lot of light in some of them. And some of them were made of stone on the outside, which I thought was really beautiful. They didn't have stained glass, though. The good thing was that the crosses were just plain crosses, with no Jesus hanging on them.

I went to a Jewish synagogue also, but I felt funny going there with Roxie, because we weren't Jewish. We weren't Christian either, of course, but we could have been, because my parents were Christian, even if I didn't want to be Christian. But even though my parents were Christian, said they were Christian, they didn't go to church ever, except for weddings and funerals and stuff.

So, going [illegible] was something to do, something to see. We could walk around neighborhoods and look at different kinds of houses, too.

I went on the welfare after Do Wrong Ron left, and then, when Roxie was five and went to kindergarten, I got a job in a supermarket, but it didn't pay enough, so I moved back in with my parents, back in my old bedroom, with Roxie. And since my mom didn't work, she took care of Roxie. She was a good mother, so she was a good grandmother too.

I wanted to go to college. I saved a bunch of money working in the supermarket, and when I could, I went to a state college part-time. They took me because my grades in high school were really good—except for English, but even the English grades weren't really bad, just not as good as anything else. It took me eight years, but I studied education and art, and I graduated, and I qualified to take a state licensing exam in teaching, and, back then, the schools still taught art and still hired art teachers, and I was lucky and got a job in a middle school pretty near where we lived. I still teach there.

Sounds good, right? Something went wrong. Well, you know

something woulda gone wrong, otherwise, what would I have to tell about?

When Roxie was 10 years old, Do Wrong Ron had a stroke, and became an invalid. He was "incapacitated". And, since we never divorced, guess what? I was responsible for him. I went to Family Court and argued about it, but I couldn't afford a lawyer, my parents couldn't afford a lawyer, and even though he never paid child support or anything, never supported Roxie, never visited her, I had to pay part of my salary toward his "upkeep". It was court-mandated. So I did. I didn't visit him, didn't go to see how "incapacitated" he was, because, coulda woulda shoulda, I might really have murdered him. If he were truly incapacitated, I coulda woulda shoulda smothered him with a pillow. If he weren't, I coulda woulda shoulda gone back to court.

So all that nice money I was earning, money enough for me to live on in my own apartment, wasn't so nice after all, since enough of it went to Do Wrong Ron, and I had to keep living with my parents. Which was okay. I guess. We all got along. I just didn't feel grown up the way I wanted to feel, though.

I read more Zen koans, though, and other books about Zen. And I learned I had to find answers on my own, from within, not from others. Which I kinda knew anyway, because I sure knew enough not to go to church. So did my parents, you know. They knew there were no answers there. They told me to read read read. They told me there was a lot of wisdom in books, and I would change—for the good, for the better—if I read. And so I read.

And Roxie read. All those visits to the library really were great. She loved reading. She loved books. And, since the library had so many kinds of books, I could teach her about art from books. So she loved art. And, since the library had so many records you could borrow, I saved up and bought a little hi-fi, with a radio and a record player, and we listened to all kinds of music. Not just the popular music—not just "doo ron ron ron, de doo ron ron", all kinds. Classical music. Blues music. Folk music. Pete Seeger and Joan Baez and Bob Dylan. And we danced all the time.

Is this a good story or a bad story? Does it have a happy ending or a sad ending? It's not over. You can skip to the end, but you won't get to the end of the story. If I'm telling it, well, then, obviously, it's not over.

Anyway – Reader, I was a school teacher, and Roxie was doing well in school, and my parents and I got along, and my two sisters and my brother, all older than me, were happy, and then –

One Friday night I went to a free concert of folk music in a public park about a half mile away from where I lived, and it was terrific, and the audience sang along, and I sang along, and I met this guy. This guy. He was sitting right next to me. I was alone, and he was alone. And we both were singing along. I could hear him singing along, and he could hear me.

He had a really sweet voice. There was an intermission, and lots of people were getting up to buy stuff from an ice cream vendor and other stuff to eat also, but we didn't. He turned to me, and we began to talk about music. He played the guitar and the banjo, he said, and even a little mandolin, and told me I had a really nice voice – well, I do, and I love to sing – and he suggested we could get together and sing folk music together. He was really considerate and polite. He said that since we didn't know each other, I might not be comfortable going to his apartment, and since I might not be comfortable having him come to where I live, we could meet in the park during the day, on the weekend, and sing there.

I said yes.

So we went to the park one weekend, sang together, and of course eventually we started really dating, and, guess what –

Reader, I married him.

But that's not the end of the story.

Do you want to know his name? His name is Randolph. No one calls him Randolph, not even his parents. Everyone calls him Randy.

We got married, and Roxie and my parents really loved him, and still do, and of course we moved in together, he left his apartment, and I moved out of my parents' house, and we found a really nice apartment together, near the park.

Guess what? He's a college teacher. Not just a regular teacher, a college teacher. And he thinks I'm smart enough for him. Guess what he teaches? Music.

Together, we developed a repertoire of old ballads, English and Irish and Scottish and Appalachian and Ozark Mountains ballads. And other folk music too. And we began to sing in clubs together. Rosie and Randy. People came, and we made extra money, and we were so happy.

When Roxie grew up, she started a singing career too. She has a group called Roxanne and Roll. When they sing "Proud Mary" together, and come to the chorus, and sing, "Rollin' down the river", everyone just screams. For a while, she dated a guy from the Roll, and his name was John, and they would sing, "Roll On John" -- "Well, roll on John, and take your time, I done broke down, and I can't take mine", and everyone would scream. And, of course, "Roll in My Sweet Baby's Arms" always got a laugh. "Roll Over, Beethoven", Chuck Berry. "Roll Me Away", Bob Seger. So Roxanne and Roll are really rockin' it. "Rock and Roll is Here to Stay", Danny and the Juniors told us, and it looks like they are right.

And folk music is here to stay too.

Oh, Reader, about that support payment to Do Wrong Ron... so I got a divorce, and got married, and then we hired a private detective, and got all kinds of video footage of Do Wrong Ron dancing up a storm in clubs, and out playing B-ball with some guys in a schoolyard – and he's no kid, you know, he's got a grown up daughter, Roxie, with her own rock and roll band, he's an old guy. Well, not old old, but no kid. So, guess what, I don't pay him any more support money for his disability and incapacity. Ha! I coulda woulda shoulda maybe sued for the money back, but he doesn't have real money, so, no, not worth my time.

You can try to find videos of Randy and me singing on YouTube. Rosie and Randy, we are.

Two of my favorite songs of ours are old folk songs, "All My Troubles", and "Troubled in Mind". "If religion was a thing that money could buy, the rich would live and the poor would die, all my troubles, Lord, soon be over." Well, none of us ever has no troubles, because trouble is part of life. "Troubled in mind, and I'm blue, but I won't be blue always, cause the sun gonna shine in my back door some day."

Okay, when I met Do Wrong Ron, there wasn't a song out called "I Knew You Were Trouble", Taylor Swift, so I didn't know enough not to get in trouble with him. Then, later, there was a song, "Bridge Over Troubled Water", Paul Simon, and that was Randy.

Reader, this time, the real true ending – only, it's not an ending, I'm just not writing this any more – So, I fooled you. If you skipped to the end, guess what you would read --

Reader, I married him.

Chapter Five
I WANT TO READ, AND WRITE, AND LEARN

Once upon a time I believed in my heart and soul that reading and writing and learning was magic. I was very young.

I am old now. And I still believe....

I was born in 1910, in Poland, in a small village, what we called a "shtetl", outside of Warsaw, and then, before I turned five, we moved to Warsaw, just as World War I began. "Shtetl". Shtetl is a Yiddish word. We were Jews. I was the first-born child.

We were very very poor.

My mother had three more babies there. Little baby boys. And all three died, of malnutrition. Essentially, of starvation. And my mother's heart broke over and over, in many many pieces. Her heart never healed.

No food. Sometimes my mother would give me an empty soup pot, and I would carry it through the streets, and up a hill, to the Big House, where rich people lived. They had food. I went around back to the kitchen door, and asked for scraps. The woman there put their onion skins, and potato peelings, and carrot peelings, and green pea pods, into the soup pot, and I would bring it home, and my mother would make soup, and we would eat soup. It was hot, and smelled good.

In 1920, when my mother was pregnant again, my father went to America, so no more babies would die. When he earned enough money, he sent for my mother and me. I was 10 years old. We got to America. I stood on the deck of the ship, looking and looking until I saw the "Lady", the statue of the "Lady". My mother told me that when we saw the "Lady", we would be in America, and the "Lady" would take care of us. I found out she also was called the Statue of Liberty. We went to live with other Jews, like a big shtetl in an even bigger shtetl, in New York City. My mother had the baby there, my brother Binyamin, and two years later, my sister Zipporah.

They didn't die.

When we lived in Warsaw I wanted to learn to read and write.

But I was Jewish. I didn't think the real Polish people would let a Jew come and learn in their school, so I made up a Polish-sounding name, that wasn't Jewish-sounding like my name, and I practiced speaking like a real Polish person, and then I went to the school and told them my Polish-sounding name, and they wrote my name down and I was in a class with all real Polish children, and I learned to read and write. I was so scared they would find out I was Jewish, and would put me in jail for lying, for stealing real Polish school, so I studied so hard, and I learned, I learned, I learned, and after six weeks, when I knew I could read and write Polish, one day I never went back to school, and didn't go to jail.

But I also wanted to learn to read and write Yiddish. Jewish children could go to Jewish schools, run by Jewish people, but we had to pay money to go, and we didn't have money. Poland was in a war, lots of countries were in a war, which is why we never had enough money, or enough food. After my last baby brother died, I started taking a groszy from my mother's little purse every now and then, until I saved enough for Jewish school. I went as long as my money lasted, also six weeks, long enough to learn to read and write Yiddish, but I was afraid to take any more money, so I stopped going after that.

How I Learned About Prejudice

My father had gone to America, die Goldene Medina, the Golden Land, where it was safe to be Jewish, and where people could live without their babies starving to death, to work, to earn enough money to bring my mother and me to die Goldene Medina to live there with him. He worked, and sent the money, and we sold as much of our furniture as we could, and gave the rest away, and put our clothing in two small carpetbags, and boarded a train at the Vienna Station. We were in a third-class carriage and we were going to go all the way across Europe to France, to Le Havre, to go on a ship. We had some food with us, bread and an onion and a turnip. We sat with our carpetbags all crushed together with other people. The train stopped at a lot of other stations. At one station in Poland, a group of young, handsome Polish soldiers got on. They were drunk. I had never seen a group of drunk teenaged boys before. They were noisy, they sang songs, they were rough. They saw my mother and me, and one soldier said, "It stinks in here! Doesn't it stink in here?" And all the boys laughed and said, "Yes, it stinks in here!" Then the same soldier said, "I smell Zhids. That's why it stinks so bad. The dirty Zhids are stinking up the train!" And he walked over to us and said, "Let's throw the dirty Zhids off the train. They stink up everything!" And then they grabbed my mother, and me, and began dragging us toward the door.

Oh, the train was going fast, so fast, so fast. I didn't know if they could open the door. But if they could, and they threw us off, I knew we would die. I would die, my mother would die, and the baby inside her would die. All three of us would die. I began to cry.

Would they throw us off? Would they really? They were laughing. Was it just a joke? Or did they mean it? I didn't know. I thought I would die. Mammale, Mammale, I don't want to die....

And then a few men began to yell at the soldiers. "Shame on you, boys, shame on you, big strong men like you grabbing a pregnant woman and a little girl, and dragging them around! Shame on you! That is not what they teach in our glorious Polish army! For shame!"

The soldiers looked ashamed. They let go of us. Mamma and I ran back to where we had been sitting, and our carpetbags were still there, still safe, no one stole any of our clothing, or our food. My mother was shaking. Her whole body was shaking. She held me very close to her, very tight against her body, and we held on to each other. No one said anything to us. I think everyone was still afraid of the soldiers, they didn't want the soldiers to notice them. The train kept speeding along.

Hours and hours passed. The train began to slow down again. I wondered if we were in France already. But no, we still had a long way to go. I wanted to be in France already, but we were stopping right at the Polish and German border. All the drunken Polish soldier boys got off, and everybody seemed more relaxed. And then, a group of drunken young German soldiers got on the train.

No, no, no. Oy, Mammale. Gevalt. Now what will happen?

The drunken German soldiers were laughing, and singing,

and talking in German. German sounds a little like Yiddish, so I understood some of what they were saying—and some of what they were saying wasn't very nice.

There was a young Polish Christian girl traveling alone. She had sat very quietly for hours on end. She had long blonde hair, which was braided and wrapped like a coronet around her head, so she looked like she was wearing a golden crown. She looked like a princess. How old could she have been? Then I thought she was eighteen years old, and I think I was probably right.

One of the German soldiers noticed her, and walked over to her, and said something very rude about her body. He said she was schöne. We say shaine in Yiddish, but I knew what he meant. Telling her she was pretty wasn't rude, but telling her what he was going to do to her body with his hands was very rude. And he dragged her up on her feet and began grabbing at her body, and the other soldiers surrounded them, and a few of them grabbed too, and she was crying and begging them to stop. My mother kept hugging me and trying to hide me with her body.

Then some men on the train started yelling at the soldiers. In German. Some of the men were Polish, but they spoke German. And there were German men there too, and they were yelling. The men yelled, "Shame on you, boys, shame on you! Have you no decency? Have you no shame? Don't you have sisters, or a mother, or girl cousins? Do you want them to be treated like this? Let her go!" The German soldiers just laughed. For a minute. Then they stopped. Some of the older women sitting there took the girl to sit with them, and wiped her tears with the corner of their skirts, and hugged her, and told her she was a good girl.

What did I learn? I learned something I never read about anywhere, not before, not later, not years later, not when I got to be as old as I am today. This is what I learned:

I learned that anyone, whatever religion or nationality, could be a victim of other people, or could be a bully who would victimize an innocent person. It didn't matter what their background was. No one nationality or religion was people who were only bullies, and no one nationality or religion was people who were only victims.

That was one of the most important lessons anyone could learn.

I wish I could have written about this in a book, or in a newspaper, so that others could learn this too. But even if I write anything down—and I do—it never will be a book or in a newspaper. I just write it down for myself, because I am so happy I learned to read and write. Because I learned to read and write, I learned to learn....

Or maybe, I learned to learn because I lived....

I live to learn and I learn to live....

I tell people what I learned, though. I talk about this with friends, and with family members. With young people, very young people. I want all young people to learn, to learn to love and respect all people, so that they never will behave like any of those drunken soldiers.

The train ride didn't last forever, even though what I learned did last, and will last forever, until I die, and even then, because I taught so many people about what I learned, it might get passed on, it might last forever. Anyway, the train ride didn't last forever, we got to France, we got to Le Havre, we went aboard a big boat called a ship.

I don't want to talk about being on the ship. I hated it. A lot of people were crammed onto the ship. Some slept downstairs, way downstairs, and some slept on the deck, on the wooden floors of the deck, the dirty floors. My mother and I slept on the deck. The ocean spray got us wet. Sometimes, when it rained, everyone on the deck tried to press against the outside walls of the cabins, where we couldn't go, trying to get under the little protruding eaves, trying to stay dryer than we would if we just stayed where we were sitting or lying around on the deck.

I don't want to tell you about what it felt like when we had to urinate or defecate, where we had to go, what we had to do, what it looked like and smelled like. I won't tell you. I don't want to remember. I guess this is what learning to read and write is about, telling people the truth about the world, but even though what happened is true, it's too disgusting, I don't want to talk about it.

I don't want to talk about what happened when people got seasick.

We traveled for more than a month. We all were so dirty.

So, never mind.

Freedom and Prejudice

We crossed the whole entire Atlantic Ocean and came to New York City, America. My mother told me to look for the Lady With the Lamp, that she was a beautiful giant, shining like silver, and she was very kind, she was Freedom. My mother kept saying, "Look for the Lady". I looked and looked. I saw land. I saw tall tall buildings. I saw the Lady. She was very beautiful. But she wasn't a real human lady. She was a great big giant statue. I had thought she was a human lady, I was so excited about seeing a giant human lady who was real Freedom. So, I was disappointed. But I was happy too, because she was very special, a very special statue, and we were in America now, and we were going to be free.

I didn't know then that once upon a time there were Negroes in America who were slaves, who weren't free, and that now those Negroes weren't slaves any more, but they weren't free the way white people were, they couldn't sit where they wanted to on a bus or a train, or in a movie theater, they had to sit in something called the "Colored Section".

That was wrong. In where my mother and I came from, if we went from Poland into Germany, if we got off a train in a German train station, we would have to go to a special section also, a special waiting room section for "Östenjuden", Eastern Jews, Jews who weren't German Jews, Jews from Poland and Russia and places like that, Eastern Jews. But I never got off the train we were on when we stopped at German stations, so I never had to go to the special section. I knew, though, that I couldn't go to the regular waiting room for regular people, people who weren't Östenjuden like us. So I knew what Negroes felt when they had to go to Colored sections, and use Colored water fountains, because they weren't regular people like white people. Only white people were regular people. It took me a long time to understand that even though I was Jewish, and didn't know English yet, and looked very different from other people in New York City, that my clothes were so different, I was still regular people, because I was white.

But even then, I wasn't really regular people like white people, because there were a lot of places Jews weren't allowed to live.

Negro people couldn't live anywhere where white people lived, they always lived only in neighborhoods were only Negro people lived, but there were some places where regular white people who weren't Jewish lived, where white Jewish people still could live, and some places where Jews were not allowed to live anyway.

I learned that America was not fair to Negro people at all, and sometimes not fair to Jews.

In America, in New York City, I could go to school. They taught everything in English. I didn't know English. the words all sounded like glbyl yaga gla gla dib nah brah. But I learned to understand English, and I learned to read and write English.

I wanted to read and write.

The school gave me books to take home and read and bring back again. I read them. I heard about a library with books where I could go and borrow a book and read it at home, and bring it back to the library, and I did that too.

I learned a lot more than just plain old reading and writing. I learned to think. I wanted to understand the world, the strange world, the world where people fought wars, where people died in the wars, where babies died of starvation, where some people didn't like other people, where a lot of people didn't like Jews.

I liked what I learned about America, what America said it believed in. America believed in equality, in freedom for all people, in fairness. America had a Constitution. I read the Constitution. I believed in the Constitution.

And then I learned that America was only fair for some people, but not for everyone. America had slaves once.

I learned about the oppression of Negroes, black people stolen from Africa and brought across the Atlantic Ocean to the New World, where they were sold as slaves, where they didn't have any rights, where they were oppressed. I learned that there were people with white skin and people with black skin and people with yellow skin and people with red skin—much much later I learned about people with brown skin too—and I learned that people with white skin thought that people with black and yellow and red skin were inferior. I learned about prejudice. I learned that prejudice meant pre-judging, forming assumptions about people based on superficial reasons, before you really knew anything at all about who a person actually was. I learned that certain people were discriminated against—Negro people—and Jews. Jews like me. And I realized that I already knew everything about prejudice, and how awful and stupid and evil prejudice is.

In New York City, America, I saw my father again. He came to find us. First Mamma and I went to Ellis Island, and we were lucky, because we weren't sick, so we wouldn't be sent back on another ship, away from America, we could stay. We went home with Tata, my father, to a little apartment, where there was running water, where we could get clean, and my Tata had clean clothes for Mamma and me. And there were toilets too, outdoors in the back, shared with other families, but so much nicer than what we did on the ship. But I don't want to remember the ship, remember? So we won't talk about that.

Mamma had her baby. And the baby stayed alive. Mamma had milk inside her body, good milk, enough milk. And later, because Mamma and Tata were together again, she had another baby. I had a brother, and then a sister, and both babies stayed alive, and became children, and then grown-ups. They stayed alive, and I loved them, and they loved me.

But my mother got sick, and went to the hospital, and never came back. She died.

I was in school, and I learned to read and write English, and began to write stories in English, and my teachers told me my stories were wonderful. They were true stories. What's the difference between a true story and a made-up story? I don't think there is a difference. Made-up stories have made-up names, not the names of real people, but the stories sometimes are true anyway.

I wished my stories could be in a book, like the books I was reading. But I was just a kid.

I had a mother and a father, and a little brother and a baby sister, and I wrote stories, and then my mother went away and never came back, my mother died. The welfare ladies came to take my brother and sister and put them in a special home for little children who didn't have a mother. I said I would take care of them, but they said I was too young. Later, my father found a new wife, and she didn't have any children, and they took my sister and brother back again, but by then I had moved out of the house, I couldn't live there with that new wife, because she wasn't my mother.

I got work cleaning people's houses, and I met people who talked to me and gave me new kinds of books to read. I read all sorts of things, and I met all sorts of people.

I met people who were Communists, who told me about how things weren't fair all over the world, and that we had to work together in solidarity with all working people all over the world, to make things fair for all people. I was 16 years old. They showed me a new newspaper, called The Daily Worker, and told me to sell it on street corners for the Communist Party, and I did. I always read everything in the newspaper, and then I sold the one I read also, because I turned the pages very carefully, so the newspaper would still look new.

I couldn't let myself be sad about my mother. I couldn't miss her. I didn't know how to cry. My mother didn't know how to cry. Her three babies in Poland died and I never saw her cry. Her two more babies in America didn't die, they lived, and they were healthy, they were strong, they laughed, they were going to grow up, I was growing up, but my mother never looked happy. She looked at them like they were going to die. She didn't look at me like that, though. She believed I was going to live.

Sometimes I thought she thought I was the real her, I was her, I would take over living for her, I would live for both of us. She didn't seem to want to live for herself. She wanted to live for me to live, and I was supposed to live for her. I was supposed to live.

But my baby brother and my baby sister might live or might die, my mother wasn't sure. They had enough milk from her, and when they got older, they had enough food, we all had enough food, Mamma and Tata and Binyamin and Zipporah and me. Food. Good food.

Bread, so much bread. Soft challah bread for Shabbos. Real soup. Not soup from potato peelings and green pea pods, kitchen scraps from other people's kitchens. Real food, whole potatoes cut up, onions cut up, carrots cut up. And, on Shabbos, with chicken.

Chicken soup.

I loved my mother. I loved to hug her. Sometimes, she looked so sad, so lonely, so all alone lonely, and I would hug her, and she would hug me, but she had this strange empty look on her face when she hugged me. Not even like she was far away. Sometimes she looked like she was far away. But when she hugged me, or Binyamin, or Zipporah, she looked strange and empty.

She went to the hospital, and the little children were taken away for a long time, and I couldn't miss her, or them. I couldn't cry. I couldn't go to school, though. I had to go to work, to clean people's houses. I missed going to school. When I was alone, and I thought about school, I cried.

But I read books, and then I didn't have to cry. Some of the people I worked for told me I was smart, and gave me books to read. Some of the books were on loan, and some were gifts. I also kept going to the library to borrow books.

The Communists I met loved to talk, and argue, and read, and argue, and talk. And some listened to music, to classical music, which I learned was the music of the ruling class, written by special musicians for money, and played by special musicians for money in people's houses or concert halls, but was very beautiful, and so we listened to it anyway. And some listened to folk music, which I learned was music that arose from the common people, the workers and farmers, not the music of the ruling class. Some of those songs were labor union songs. And a few were Yiddish songs.

Sometimes when I heard Yiddish songs I started to cry a little, because my mother never learned English, she only spoke Yiddish, she refused to speak Polish, she said she hated the Polish language. There's a special Yiddish word, "mammaloschen", mother-tongue, your natural language. Tongue and language mean the same thing. Tongue of course is a part of your body, a part that you use to make sounds, to make words. The English word "language" comes from an old word from another language, another time, a word that meant tongue, just like tongue means the body part and language, just like "loschen" means.

Other people around me spoke Yiddish all the time. My father, my neighbors, storekeepers, all spoke Yiddish, and I didn't cry.

Only Yiddish songs made me cry. My mother sometimes sang Yiddish songs, and when she did, she cried. When she sang Yiddish lullabies to Binyamin and Zipporah, she cried. She didn't make crying sounds, but tears rolled down her cheeks.

Later, when Binyamin and Zipporah came home from where the welfare ladies took them, they had new names—Benny and Susie. That's what I called them. I went to live with some Communist friends, but I came to visit Benny and Susie, and I would sing Yiddish songs to them, and big tears would roll down my cheeks.

Benny and Susie went to regular American school, and learned to read and write in English, and no one was teaching them how to read and write in Yiddish. So when I came to visit them, I taught them. I read them stories by famous Yiddish writers, and taught them how to read them for themselves. We would read funny stories, and laugh. The funny stories were about Jews who lived where I once lived, across the Atlantic Ocean, where Benny and Susie had never lived, so they learned about how I lived when I was as little as they were.

Even though I was a Communist, and against religion and superstition, sometimes I would take a subway train and travel very far, and then walk very far, in order to go to the cemetery and visit my mother's grave. When I got there, I would put a rock on her gravestone, so people would know that someone came to visit her. My father didn't visit her, because his new wife didn't want him to. No one went but me. I put a rock for me, and a rock for him, and two small pebbles for Benny and Susie, and then I would read stories out loud, making believe she could hear them. I read her some of the stories I wrote in English when I still went to school, and some I even wrote afterward, all kept in a composition notebook like you have in school, and I read her some Yiddish stories, imagining the funny ones would make her laugh and the sad ones would make her cry.

But I didn't miss her, and I didn't cry for her. I just wanted to—I don't know—I wanted to make believe she could hear me. I wanted her to hear me.

She was proud that I could read and write Yiddish, and English too! She didn't care about Polish, and I stopped caring about

Polish, and then I forgot all the Polish. She wanted me to read and write English, and I wanted to also, and now I do.

I learned magic. I was a Communist, and I was against religion and superstition, but I learned reading and writing, and reading and writing are magic. They are magic carpets. They take you away into other worlds, far away....

My mother sang a song she learned in Poland, but it wasn't a Polish song, it was a Jewish song, a Yiddish song, about children learning to read. It is called "Oyfn Pripetchik", which means "By the Little Stove". In Poland, the stoves were not like the stoves we had in America. They were little tile stoves with real burning fire – when we could build a fire, when we had money for wood to build a fire, to cook the soup and keep the room warm. We only had one room.

The song says, "Oyfin pripetchik, brent a feyerl, und der shtieb is heis, und der rebbe lernt kleine kinderlach dem alef-beis." This means, "By the stove a little fire burns, and the house is warm, and the rebbe teaches little children the alef-beis". Rebbe is the teacher, and alef-beis is the alphabet, the first two letters of the alphabet in Yiddish, Also in Hebrew, which is what the little boys learned, what the grown-up men knew, when they went to shul to pray. The prayers are in Hebrew.

Then the song says, "Zet zhe kinderlach, gedenkt zhe, tayereh, vos ir lerent do, zogt zhe nochamol, und takhe nochamol, khumetz, alef, O!"

This means, "Look now, children, remember, dears, what you are learning here, say it again, and say it again, khumetz, alef, O". Khumetz alef O is hard to explain. Alef is that first letter of the alef-beis, the alphabet, just like in English, like the letter "A". Or more like "Ah". But you could say that "A" a number of ways, and you learn about little marks that go under the letter to tell you how to pronounce it. Khumetz is a little mark that goes under the alef to give it the sound of O. I know A is A, but an alef in Yiddish, and in Hebrew too, sounds like an O when it has a khumetz sign under it. The khumetz sign looks like two dots next to each other right under the alef.

There's more words to the song, and the words get sadder

and sadder, about how sad everything in the world is. The words contradict themselves. The song says that the man who learns to read and study Torah is happy, but that when the children who are learning the song grow older, every letter and word is full of pain, and will cause tears to fall. How could that be, I wondered. How could we be happy to learn to read, to read the Torah when we are grown up, but that the words are full of pain and make us cry?

I won't write the whole song out now, just the little part about being sad: "Ir velt, kinder, elter vern, vet ihr aleyn farshteyn, vifel in der oyses ligen treyrn, un vi fil geveyn."

I wondered. But now I think I know.

I always wondered why my mother never tried to teach me to read and write Yiddish when we lived in Poland. She loved reading and writing. I wondered.

But now I think I know.

Her heart was crying for the dying children. All a child needed to do was live. Reading and writing didn't matter if a child was dying.

I didn't die. I lived. And every word we learn is filled with pain. If we understand, our eyes fill with tears.

I know....

Chapter Six
STREET SONGS

Miss Mary Mack Mack Mack

She went upstairs upstairs upstairs

To fix her bed bed bed

And hit her head head head

On a piece of cheese cheese cheese

Street games. Children singing. In the alley, no more than half drunk, Rudy hauling out the garbage cans, singing too.

Zekiel saw the wheel

Way up in the middle of the air

Zekiel saw the wheel

Way in the middle of the air.

The man is hardly bigger than the children. His left leg is twisted, but he can move around okay, for a cripple. He's going to be drunk by nightfall, and he'll tell you that too, if you stop to talk. He likes to talk, but there's no one much to talk to, now they took Lightnin' away.

Big wheel run by faith

Little wheel run by the grace of God

Wheel in a wheel

Way in the middle of the air.

Lightnin'. His room was in the back, on the courtyard, and was dark. People who had been inside, and they were few, said it was filled with nothing but junk. There were six padlocks on his door. Essie, who looked in on him from time to time in the weak-sunned winter months, would tell him to clean up the mess. He would turn his yellow eyes on her and tell her to git, that wasn't no mess, that was the way he liked it, and he was living his own life. She'd stand there shaking her head and pursing her lips, eying the junk, and then would ask him if there was anything he needed. He'd roar that anything he needed he could get, except one thing, and that would come in time. What you need, Lightnin'? I need the sun, girl, that's all I need. Essie would laugh, and then go home to those who needed her. After she'd gone, Lightnin' would move about his room, feeling dissatisfied, trying to see the mess. No matter how hard he looked he couldn't find it. It just wasn't there.

Lightnin's room. Old photographs and magazine cut-outs taped to the walls, the largest picture directly over his bed, a glossy eight by ten, cracked, showing a much younger Lightnin' at a piano, grinning, two horns, a bass, and a guitar grinning back. On a battered kitchen table and a rolltop desk nearby were scattered tin cans serving as ashtrays, candle holders, catch-alls for nuts, screws, bolts, nails, odds and ends. Among the welter of broken alarm clocks, radios, box cameras, and other salvaged wreckage were strewn his few tools, also discards. The floor was covered with dusty carpet remnants betraying more worn spots than pattern. His mattress was set upon a wooden platform, covered and curtained with scraps. Most of the floor space was taken up by the keyboard and intestines of an old piano, the remaining shreds of wood hacked off and stacked against the walls along with the other lumber, newspapers, broken chairs that were Essie's mess.

The gas and electric were shut off, and both oven and refrigerator served as file cabinets, holding birdcages, breadboxes, bicycle pumps, whatever. Lightnin' surveyed the room, seeking what Essie saw, feeling restless, uncomfortable, as if something were missing, seeing only his home, the end of seventy-odd years of hard living.

To dispel the dissatisfaction, he would begin to tinker, to work, restoring the alarm to a clock, crackling reception to a transistor radio, patching an inner tube, setting wheels to motion once more. When peace returned, he would lie on the bed, staring at the photograph of the boldly grinning piano player, playing the Reverend Doctor Martin Luther King's speeches on a battery-run record player, humming along in a dusty voice the music that fit the words.

Later, as dark fell, he would light candles and listen to music, old records with eternally young sounds, the voices of the dead, and new voices still young, with a rawer more deadly anger to their art.

The wheel turned and Lightnin' lived out another winter, emerging into the spring, to greet the sun and set up housekeeping outdoors, his chairs, brooms, phonograph, cartons of lunch and supper alongside the tenement building like a gypsy caravan at the side of a populous village. He would sweep his land morning and evening, doze in the sun, drink a little under the moon, his phonograph enlightening a drowsy neighborhood, the voice of the Reverend Doctor Martin Luther King, the horn of Miles Davis, the piano of Meade Lux Lewis bringing it all back home. As the sun strengthened, so did Lightnin', his gypsy camp and blaring music lasting all day and half the night until one, two in the morning, when he would pack up and move indoors to sleep, re-emerging with the rising sun.

Late Saturday nights he would bathe and early Sunday mornings he would appear, dressed in a well-pressed suit, his hickory walking stick richly oiled, his shoes shined, a Panama hat covering his close-clipped grizzled hair. If the weather were fine he'd parade up and down the street, pausing at the corner across from the park to rest, inspecting his street, his land, as if he were squire and the people his people, and he would smile graciously upon all. Then he'd stalk off, leaning heavily on his cane, to be gone a few hours, reappearing in the afternoons to sit with a few cronies, mostly old men like crippled Rudy, although a few young men, broad-shouldered and bad in black mesh shirts, would sit with them on the garbage cans and parked cars. There they would drink and tell stories, their voices lowered, and laugh loud.

Now there were some folk who thought he went to church in those lost hours, and some who swore he was too much a renegade to do any such thing. At any rate, Sundays he would walk out in his fine suit with his cane newly oiled to disappear into the city for a few hours before coming home to drink and talk. Mondays he would be back with all his junk, battered easy chairs dragged from the cellar, cartons and brooms and rags, wearing baggy pants shiny with age, his toes wriggling in his cut-out carpet slippers, an old overcoat, definitely unpressed, draped over his chair, to sport an assortment of unlikely hats during the rest of the week, women's flower-bedecked hats, sombreros, hats feathered, tasseled, fringed, sheltering his bald spot from the sun.

The seasons changed for him, the children shot up into long-legged adolescents, new little ones played with old tricycles and sang the street songs, old tenants moved out and new tenants moved in, old men and women were carried away by ambulance to city hospitals and they never came back, love affairs blossomed, marriages died, Essie continued to look in winters and the old men chatted with him summers, and Lightnin' grew old, locked into the seasons, the turning of the wheel.

One spring things were different. The wheel within the wheel started spinning, out of rhythm, a new sound, a new grace, a new life for an old man. From out of his room Lightnin' dragged the wreckage of his piano, and cast it to the four winds, to seek an older way of life, a deeper memory. Somewhere in the granite city he found tools, old and rusty, a hoe, a rake, a spade. Next to the alley running alongside the apartment building was a fence. From the fence a slope of earth led down to train tracks that wound in the open a mile or two before disappearing underground. The fence was one day ripped open, so that a man of over six feet, weighing just short of two hundred pounds, could walk through, carrying old and rusty tools, could walk upon the weedy slope of earth.

Lightnin' worked hard from early spring, hunched against the March chill in his shabby overcoat, discarding it as labor brought sweat to his brow. From scraps of lumber he built a shack, furnishing it with castoffs dragged from cellars, padlocking it against vandals and street arabs, a shack to store his tools in. When the shack was built he began to dig, a bent brown giant sculpting earth, creating a terrace farm from the edge of the train track to the ruined wire fence. He planted tomatoes, tying the plants to sticks to bear the weight of the heavy fruit. He planted corn and beans in the rich earth high on the slope, and lettuce and spinach in the sandier earth at the bottom near the tracks. He weeded the garden, eating dandelion greens with his supper. He labored for hours beneath the waxing summer sun, and though he bent over his garden all day he seemed straighter in the early evening cool, taller and stronger and lustier. Some folk thought he was seeing a woman on his lost Sunday afternoons, he looked so upbeat.

And his garden grew. He built fires in the evening, and boiled beans in July, roasted young ears of corn in early August. After his evening meal he would climb a ladder to the roof of his shack, and play records on his portable phonograph. The voice of the newly-dead Reverend Doctor Martin Luther King proclaiming his dream once more to the open sky, the long-silenced roll of the piano of Meade Lux Lewis, the clear black ice of the horn of Miles Davis, the sounds of decades of music resurrected beneath the night sky sang in the garden of the old man. And there were those who heard the sounds bitter and sweet driving away ghosts in the night and were gladdened by it, and there were those who tossed unhappy and afraid, unable to sleep and soundly angered.

Several nights one week a patrol car drove up the street, stopping before the railroad tracks, and two young slim men, crisp in blue, would jump out and saunter up to the fence. Lightnin' would turn low the phonograph, scramble down his ladder, and just as jauntily saunter up to the men. Hey Pop, people are complaining here, say they can't sleep. No, is that right? All they got to do is ask me, I'll turn it down low. How things going? Everything cool, no trouble? That's good, that's good. You drive on now, I'll keep this thing real low. Okay Pop, take it easy, and keep that thing low, people got a right to sleep. The two young men would jump back in their car and drive around the corner to the used car lot where they would coop, catching a nap undisturbed by the old man's music, while Lightnin' would climb back up his ladder and listen to the low sounds, low and bitter, low and sweet.

The next week the squad car came more often, and in the days too, with two older burlier cops, who would ease out the door and swagger to the fence and call Hey Lightnin', you making any trouble? The old man would rest on his hoe and call back Who me? I never make trouble, boss, I am the mayor of this here street. I keep trouble away. You show me where's the trouble at, and old Lightnin' here will blast that trouble out.

Yeah Lightnin', well we don't want no trouble, you hear? Keep outa trouble now. Sure thing, boss. We don't want no trouble, no sir. The two men would walk back to the squad car and drive off, and Lightnin' would watch them drive out of sight, his yellow eyes narrowing, possibly against the sun. At the end of the week two transit cops drove out, along with a man dressed in a grey suit and carrying a black attaché case. They parked the car and walked around the back of the building, found the hole in the fence, shook their heads and slipped through. Lightnin' came out to meet them, carrying a spade in one hand. He leaned the spade against the shack, picked up his hickory stick and leaned on it, his teeth showing in what was almost a smile. When no one spoke he said Morning, gentlemen, pushing his sun hat, the one with the feather, back off his brow.

Quite a farm you have here, said the man with the attaché case. Lightnin' didn't answer, just looked around, and his hand tightened on his hickory stick.

You are aware that this is private property, the man continued, beaming a broad smile.

Thought it was city property, Lightnin' answered.

Well, yes it is, that it is, the man assented, nodding his head vigorously, still smiling.

That's what I thought. Well, I am a part of this city, have lived in this city for twenty-two years, have paid my taxes, have lived in this building right here for the last six years. Never seen the city farm this here piece of land yet. They fixin' to farm it now?

No, no, they're not. Smiling, smiling away.

Gonna do any building on this little piece of land?

No, no building. The fact is, they're not planning to do anything with it.

Well, that's good, cause I wouldn't fight the mayor over anything he wanted to do with city land. The mayor is the mayor, he is the boss, he knows what to do with this city land.

Yes, well, the city plans to leave this land alone, and you will have to do the same.

Why? Ain't it city land? I am a citizen of this city.

This ain't open to the public, mac, said one of the men in uniform. The man with the attaché case looked at him and frowned.

Mr. Bowles is right, of course. This land is not open to the public.

Why not? said Lightnin'.

Well, if everyone did what he or she wanted to do on this land and land like this, things would be in a mess, wouldn't they? Why, children might get killed playing on the track.

I'm over twenty-one, Lightnin' said.

Well, to be sure....

No one is gonna git themselves killed.

I hope not....

I'm just farming this empty land.

Ah, but everyone just can't do as he or she pleases. This is private property. Harvest what you can today, and tomorrow these two gentlemen will be back with some workmen to take down the... ah... shack....

I'll take it down, muttered Lightnin'.

I beg your pardon?

I'll take it down, Lightnin' roared, bearing down on the three men, hickory stick waving in the air, yellow eyes aglow. I'll take it down my own self. I'll rip the whole motherfuckin' thing down my own self.

Don't curse at me like that, Pop, said the man in uniform.

Nothing to argue about murmured the man with the attaché case, laying a soft hand on the transit cop's shoulder. He said he would take it down. You come out tomorrow, Mr. Bowles, see that it is down, that the area is properly cleared. Good day, sir, nodding to Lightnin'. We're sorry of course, but you must understand that if anyone were to do what he or she wanted to do... well... it wouldn't do.

The three strangers left. Lightnin' packed up the things he wanted, dragged tools and phonograph and easy chair back to his apartment, and spent the rest of the day smashing down the shack. He cried. When the shack was nothing but a mass of splintered boards he stood for a moment among the vegetables and debris, shaking his head, tears wet on his cheeks, his large body sweating and trembling all over. No sir I do not understand. I ain't gonna understand neither.

The farm turned back to wasteland. Weeds choked out the corn. Workmen had come to cart away the debris, trampling the plants. Lightnin' sat out on the garbage pails and parked cars with the other old men, drinking peach wine and telling stories, laughing loud. They argued more than was usual, but everyone agreed that it was too fuckin' hot. Lightnin' stomped up and down, banging his hickory cane, cursing heavy, grunting whenever the squad car passed, lying low. He hobbled bent over his cane, mean drunk, and raised his cane at people whenever they got in his way. Rudy tried to take him home but Lightnin' told him to get his cripple's ass out of his way or he'd twist his good leg around his neck. Rudy left him to his peach wine, to his banging his cane against the garbage cans. Later Lightnin' went home.

Then Lightnin' got it together again. He eased off the wine, put down his cane, and moved his gypsy camp. He crossed the street, abandoning the garbage cans and parked cars and the shade of his looming building and set up his easy chairs against the low stone wall shielding the railroad tracks from the sidewalk where the children played. He lay down an old piece of carpet, positioned three easy chairs, and erected a canopy out of lumber and more carpeting. He added an end table, his phonograph, and a couple of orange crates full of records that doubled as footstools, and like an Asian potentate he mounted his throne and created a court.

Beneath the patterned fantasy of pomegranates and curlicues he reigned, while youngblood courtiers in black mesh shirts, handkerchiefs knotted at their throats, sat with him. The old men, janitors and handymen, retired pensioners, joined him in his cloister, and soon their ribald jokes and bawdy laughter dominated the street. Children gathered at his feet and he suffered them and gladly. He had stories to tell, stories for little children and young men and old men too. Young women and the elderly not at all given to loud laughter and peach wine drew to the side as they passed. In the building next to his derelict court people muttered why don't he stay where he belongs? He don't live on this side of the street.

Lightnin' had acquired an empire and as emperor he regarded himself as the servant of the people. Each morning he would sweep the length of the street, both sides. After meals refuse would go in the garbage can and he would sweep his camp clean. At sunset he would sweep both sides of the street once more. In the waning summer sun he would sit in his easy chair, faded purple and golden splendor, looking across the street to where once he had a farm. Then the patrol car cruised by again, and the sergeant himself came out to see.

Lightnin', you know you can't do this.

What can't I do? They sittin' on their fancy aluminum folding chairs over there, they on the sidewalk same as me. You gonna chase me, you chase them too.

We ain't chasing you off the sidewalk, Lightnin'. You wanna sit out on a chair, you sit out on a chair. But this shit has gotta go.

What shit has gotta go?

All this shit, man. You can't turn the sidewalk into a junkyard.

I take it in with me at night. It ain't here lessen I here too, using it.

No rug, Lightnin'. No boxes, no rags, no tables, no lumber. Just a chair. The rest of this shit goes. Understand?

Okay, sergeant. I understand. How about my record player? You got a law against a record player?

Just don't play it too loud, fella.

Okay, sergeant. I won't play it too loud.

Overnight the fabulous oriental palace with its rugs, draperies, canopy, throne, disappeared. The court was dispersed, the laughter died. Everything was clean and quiet. Lightnin' stalked down the street early that morning, circled the park, sniffing the crazy smell of freshly mown grass. Oh, and he hated it, the new manicured sterility of grass that grazed no livestock, earth that grew no tomatoes, no corn, lake where no fishing was allowed. He stormed home brandishing his stick, eying the delicate old ladies and feeble old men huddled in their rows of aluminum chairs before their building, dying in the street. He muttered to himself and they shrank back, their feet drawn up beneath their chairs, and they too muttered to themselves. Someone ought to put him away somewhere. That crazy old guy is gonna hurt someone some day.

Across the street Essie put a hand to her head, patted the rows of pink hair rollers, and said to the woman standing with her, that darn crazy fool. He gonna get himself in trouble. That old fool.

One Sunday, an overripe August morning, Lightnin' came out in his Sunday best, Panama hat and oiled cane, dragging a wooden kitchen chair, with his phonograph and records. Grimly he moved across the street, into the midst of the aluminum chairs where sat the little old men and little old women sheltered from the sun beneath the shade tree that grew in front of their building. He sat down and played his Reverend Doctor Martin Luther King record, turning the volume on loud. Turn that thing down. Why don't you go sit in front of your own house? Yeah, you don't belong here. Go on back across the street. Shut that thing off. Lightnin' slit his yellow eyes, possibly against the glare of the sun on the chrome of a parked car, and softly he sang music to the words. An old woman, her eyes filled with tears, her mouth drawn in a thin line, folded her chair and went indoors. Moments later the patrol car arrived.

All right, what's the trouble here? the sergeant asked. Lightnin' sat stolidly, his Panama pulled down over his eyes, not moving, not talking. He didn't have to. The men and women sitting next to him moved and talked a lot. The sergeant listened to their animated complaints, then bellowed, All right! They all sat down again, ruffled.

Now you folks listen. You bothered this old man enough. You complained about his farm, all right, we shut down his farm. You complained about his pile of junk down by the tracks with all those fellas drinking there, all right, we closed down his pile of junk down by the tracks. Now here he is among you, on a chair like you, and there ain't nothing I'm gonna do about it. He got a right. You leave him alone, don't bother him no more, and don't bother us no more. People is getting shot in this city, and you complaining about a man doing just what you doing. He ain't breaking no laws.

But he doesn't live here, officer, ventured an old woman in a beribboned picture hat.

Neither do you, lady. You live in a house. He lives in a house. The sidewalk ain't private property. Don't call the police no more.

But I didn't call the police.

Then your girlfriend did. Leave this man alone.

Sorry you got so much trouble outta this, Sergeant, Lightnin' said.

Don't you get into any trouble, Pop.

No sir. I am the mayor of this block. I blast trouble. Lightnin' is my name and I blast trouble.

The police left.

You ought to be ashamed of yourself, bothering old ladies like this, a man said.

They ought to be ashamed of themselves, bothering me, Lightnin' answered. You heard what the sergeant said. You is bothering me. I is an old man, motherfucker. I is seventy-six years of age, and I biggern you and bettern you and strongern you. Come on, man, come on and hit me. Hit me and I'll whup you, motherfucker. It's self defense. I'll break your cocksuckin' head.

No one wants to hit you, the old woman in the picture hat said. He fell down on his knees before her, lay his head in her lap, and pointed at his neck, screaming, come on, motherfucker, come and hit me. I is seventy-six years of age. You must got twenty good years on me. Hit me and I'll whup you good.

The old woman, surprising even herself, giggled. Get up, Lightnin', no one's gonna hit you.

Get away from that woman, the other man yelled, shaking Lightnin' by the shoulder. Lightnin' sprang up. You hit me, motherfucker? It's self defense if I kill you, God help you, it's true self defense.

The man backed away, his hands before his face. I'm not fighting with you. I have a heart condition.

You busted up my garden, you busted up the place where me and my friends met. Didn't you hear about what the Reverend Doctor Martin Luther King said? Didn't you hear about that one man's dream? You heard what the sergeant said. I can sit anywhere I fuckin' please.

No one said anything about color, the woman in the picture hat said, handing Lightnin' his Panama.

No one has to say anything about color. He is white and I is black and that's color, mama. I ain't taking no more shit. No sir, motherfucker, I ain't taking no more shit.

Lightnin' stood there breathing heavily as everyone hastily folded their chairs and went home. Then he sat, with his dreams of dreams and his music, face turned to the sun. After a victorious hour, he went home too, for lunch. When he returned his kitchen chair was lying in pieces in the gutter, and the aluminum chairs were back in place. Three young men stood against the parked cars, watching him. They weren't wearing black mesh shirts, they didn't wear handkerchiefs knotted at their throats. Lightnin' took the broken chair home, and stayed home.

Rain fell Monday and Tuesday, breaking the heat wave. Seven o'clock Wednesday morning Lightnin' padlocked another kitchen chair to the fence running alongside the building beneath the shade tree. The old people emerging from the building later that morning, seeing him sitting there drinking peach wine, set their chairs up at the far end of the building.

No one, white or black, young or old, came to join Lightnin' that day. He drank steadily, listening to his records, living out on the street all day and half the night. No one called the cops. At two in the morning he called out in blurred tones, sleep tight motherfuckers, and went home. The turf he won was his. The elderly remained permanently encamped thirty yards away, and he remained in his new spot, his chair chained to the fence for the rest of the summer. After a couple of days of peach wine he remained home too sick to move, and when he came out he was wrapped in his old overcoat, although the late summer sun beat down, and he coughed steadily. His phonograph batteries ran down, and he was too feeble, or too broke, to buy more. He drank soft drinks, sat in the shady quiet, and dozed into autumn.

His old cronies, smelling frost and cold winter days in lonely rooms, sat with him as the leaves drifted down, clinging to freedom and summer. The children went back to school, the aluminum chairs were stored in closets, and a mournful serenity reigned. Soon Lightnin' alone sat in the autumn chill, bundled in his overcoat and a surplus army jacket, watching the little that was left of the summer scene. Still he swept the street, but he seemed shriveled in his victory, bereft of conflict. He grew very old.

He fought bitterly the turning of the wheel. He shouted greetings to passersby, joked with the children rushing to and from school. Then mercifully a new enemy appeared. In his absence, a dog dirtied the sidewalk where he sat, leaving a mess before his chair. Lightnin' stepped in it. Muttering in disgust, he scraped his shoe against the curb, then swept the mess away. The next morning, his cane high above his head, he chased people walking their dogs into the gutter, screaming at them to curb their dogs. The sidewalk is for the people. Git into the street with that animal. People were afraid of his yellow eyes and hard hickory stick. They walked in the gutters with their animals. He swept the street and chased dogs and dog owners, screaming, I am the mayor of this block. You got to keep this block clean. Git in the street with that dirty hound.

The wheel spun, the wheel glowed, the wheel was a fire in the mind of God. One day the wheel spun off the track, hurtled crazily away, and Lightnin' got crushed beneath it, got burned in the fire, got lost in the eternal turning of the big wheel. Down the sidewalk came a young man, broad shouldered in a black mesh shirt, a sleek Doberman at his side. Git off the sidewalk with that animal. These streets belong to the people, cried Lightnin', standing up to meet the enemy.

Aw Lightnin', sit down and behave yourself. I am the people.

Git in the gutter, motherfucker, or I'll break your head. I am mayor of this here block.

Put that cane down, man. I ain't walkin' in no gutter. My dog ain't gonna get you dirty. I'm just taking him for a walk.

Walk where you belong. Git in the gutter with that dog. Lightnin' gave the kid a shove.

Don't shove me, Lightnin'. The kid put up his hand, the dog growled, and Lightnin' shoved again. The kid shoved back and Lightnin' stumbled. Furious, he lifted his cane and as the young man walked by he brought the cane down heavy on his back. The heavy hickory stick broke right in two. The kid whirled, punched Lightnin' square in the face, and broke the old man's nose. The kid picked up the broken cane, and stood there rubbing his back, choking back his growling dog. Hell Lightnin', I didn't want to hurt you. Why'd you have to go hit me like that.

Give back my cane. Blood streamed down Lightnin's face.

You don't know what to do with no cane. You ain't gettin' it back. The kid walked off, his back and shoulder aching. Lightnin' looked around, bloody and broken, saw all the windows opening and the heads peering out. Old and beaten, he hurried home, his hands covering his face.

An hour later the kid walked home, his dog beside him. Lightnin' stepped out into the street and emptied a 16 gauge shotgun load of buckshot into the kid and his dog. The dog died. The kid fell down, the thigh bone of his left leg shattered, screaming. Lightnin' went back into the house. The street filled with people, mainly housewives and young children. Essie cradled the head of the wounded boy in her arms. What the hell got into Lightnin', the boy kept asking. Why'd he have to go shoot me for?

The police arrived before the ambulance. They asked questions, took notes, nodded gravely. The ambulance carted the young man away as eight squad car loads of policemen began to deploy themselves, guns drawn, over the street. Why don't you folks go inside. There might be shooting, someone might get hurt. Get those kids off the street, for Chrissakes. The people remained. Mothers and children remained on the street, impassive, waiting for the police to find Lightnin'. No one believed Lightnin' was going to do any more shooting. The police fanned out, covering the alleys, the rooftops, blocking off the street, roaming through hallways. They found Lightnin' huddled on a rooftop, his hands covering his broken face, blood and tears dribbling down his shirt. They led him, peaceable and handcuffed, through the hallways, through the street, past his friends and neighbors. They took Lightnin' away.

Children sing street songs.

> She called the doctor doctor doctor
>
> And he said said said
>
> If you hit your head head head
>
> On a piece of cheese cheese cheese
>
> You will die die die
>
> I'm first!

Rudy, fully drunk at nightfall, sings,

Zekiel saw the wheel
Way up in the middle of the air
Zekiel saw the wheel
Way in the middle of the air.

Children sing street songs.

I had a dream dream dream
And I did scream scream scream
Saw a man run run run
He had a gun gun gun
Gotcha!

Rudy sings.

Big wheel run by faith
Little wheel run by the grace of God
Wheel in a wheel
Way in the middle of the air.
Little wheel turn. Turn and burn.

Chapter Seven
WHAT ARE PATTERNS FOR?

> I have no refuge in this world
> other than thy threshold
> –Maksoud of Kashan
> 16th century Persian master rug weaver

Eliann was always busy. If it wasn't one thing, it was another, but mostly it was everything. The children. The baby. The house, room by room. Food. Answering bells: the door, the telephone, the timer on the dryer, the timer on the oven. Her husband. A social life. A meaningful existence. Relaxing. There always was something important to do. Eliann was always busy.

Always. It always is unfair to sum up a life, because the fact of summation ignores the always subliminal excitement of just being there, hanging out, being alive. Therefore, granting Eliann her just portion of subliminal excitement, the beating of her heart, the complicated electrochemical processes of anxiety, impatience, and ecstasy, and the fact of her immortal soul, a summation still remains accurate and moot. Eliann, a woman of the early 1970's, living in a slightly less than affluent suburb of a large northeastern American city, was a wife and mother.

Her duties were clear-cut. She cleaned her house, wiped down tile and Formica and Sanitex and linoleum, dusted plastic and wood and veneer, washed and folded cloths of many blends and many colors, cleaned ceramic and stainless steel and glass. She fetched carefully processed, pre-wrapped, already sliced, partially or wholly cooked food, prepared and served it. She kept the children clean and safe and mentally stimulated and morally fit. She planned and prepared and served feasts for large groups of people, selected the music, and made intelligent introductions. She made love like a champ, guided by her daily required reading of magazines designed to warn her what to do. She kept her body lithe and strong and responsive with TV yoga classes. And occasionally she saw things. For instance, she saw the living room rug.

One warm, rainy Thursday afternoon in October, Eliann, after dusting the wall unit and all the glossy hardcover books with dust jackets intact, the two reproduction pre-Columbian statuettes, the smoothly-glazed mass-produced vases, the onyx bookends, and the stereo, turned to her favorite household task, vacuuming. Lisa was in kindergarten, Annette was in nursery play-group, and baby Brian was fast asleep in his room at the other end of the house, so that Eliann could make all the noise she liked, zooming about the living room, sucking at the drapes, sofa, easy chairs, and, finally, the rug.

As she vacuumed she sang, something wordless and triumphant, the boldest lines of a trumpet concerto, perhaps, rambling into something ragtime, turning a quirky corner and becoming Christmas carol. Her voice faltered as she leaned her weight down the shaft of the vacuum cleaner towards the rug.

Though the cream linen drapes, chocolate brown velvet sofa, and apricot ice silken throw pillows were new and rich and beautiful, they were also bland. The rug, however, was vibrant and alive, its colors glowing from within, the patterns delicately intricate. It was an excellent and expensive copy of a Chinese rug dating from the 18th century Keen-lung period. The rug was bordered with a deep blue on the outside, then a leaf and flower motif, and then two inner borders of light blue. Designs of ripe fruit, flowers, and butterflies, in tones of deep brown, apricot, yellow, and blue were scattered upon a field of ivory. Within the central medallion, arched at the poles and triple curved at the sides, was a fruit tree, burdened with ripe apricots.

This afternoon, Eliann saw the rug. She saw the butterflies, blue and lemon, so exquisitely limned that they seemed poised in mid-flight. She saw the flowers, scattered upon the ivory field as on a meadow, so fresh that they seemed touched by sunshine. And she saw, deep within the recess of the medallion, the fat and inviting fruit of the tree. First her song trailed away, and then, as she heard the empty roar of the vacuum cleaner, she flipped the switch into silence, and stood gazing at the center of the rug.

Eliann stood gazing into the center of the rug for a long time. Something was happening. For instance, something hummed. At the center of the rug, the swirling form of the medallion and the curvilinear tree began to pulsate. At the same time, Eliann's head throbbed. She had felt her head throb with headaches before, but this throbbing was painless, even desirable. The wavering lines of the rug, the beating center, the pulse in her head, all seemed to resound silently, a silent hum. The apricot tree seemed swathed in layers of mist, as if a fog had rolled in from distant mountains. Something was happening. Eliann stood gazing into the center of the rug for a long time.

Then she shook her head, laughed at herself, and murmured aloud, "Daydreamer!" She flicked on the vacuum cleaner switch. Later, when the machine was neatly stashed away in the hall closet, she continued singing, down the hallway and into the kitchen. She plugged in the automatic coffee warmer and sang into the face of the kitchen clock.

The clock did not sing back. Its' clear plastic face stayed mute, its bronze sunburst prongs stretching silently upon the pale blue satin-finished wall. At the center two black hands met in a brilliant golden point, a point shimmering and sucking inward, in hollow silence.

It was two o'clock. It stayed two o'clock for a long time. Then it was 2:01. The golden point wavered, a thin liquid mirror about to part, to reveal something ancient and submarine. Then it was 2:20. Eliann picked up a shred of song where she had left it, something she had heard many times on the radio, bright and clear and new. She poured her cup of coffee and pulled a package of pre-formed meat patties out of the freezer to thaw. She cooled her coffee with Melloream, gulped it down, and set the pale blue Melmac cup, empty but for the dregs, upon the gold-dust-spattered cream-colored Formica counter.

Again she glanced at the clock, obliquely, keeping her eyes at the outer edges, away from the brilliant center. Half past two. Brian was sleeping later into the afternoon than was usual. Eliann stretched out into the luxury of solitude, and cast about restlessly for something to do. She poured the last half cup of coffee into her cup, and reached for the stack of magazines on the bottom tier of the tea cart, hoping to find a recipe for a special and sumptuous dessert that could be prepared in less than 15 minutes. Perhaps it was the angle of reach, or the stretch in a direction unexpected and untried, that altered her perception so drastically, but as she reached downward she noticed grease smears on the washable wallpaper that covered the wall where the electric range and wall oven were. With a sigh she stood up, wet a sponge, and knelt.

The wallpaper was a Dutch tile design of four manganese slabs, in the Louis XIV style, coming together at the corners to form a sunburst, a 16-petalled flower. Eliann swabbed at the brown-purple of the flower's heart, wearing down the resistance of grease. She rubbed and rubbed and rubbed, staring within the radiating petals, until she could no longer see grease. And yet she continued scrubbing, somewhat more slowly. And then she stopped. For quite a while she remained squatting, eyes intent upon the shimmering sunburst. At the very center of the flower she seemed to see another flower, small and perfect, a deeply blushing rose. For an instant, it seemed, she was captured by the scent of roses, more exquisite, more enticing, more intense than anything ever had been before.

Brian wailed. She glanced up at the clock. 2:53. Eliann stood up, blinking. It was nearly time for her daughters to arrive home, Annette by microbus, Lisa by yellow school bus. Eliann turned and walked out of the kitchen and down the long long hallway toward Brian's bedroom, humming a formless, aimless tune.

Many things happened. The girls came home. The television set in the family room opening onto the kitchen went on, and sang numbers bright and bold for the children to learn. "Five, five, five, five, sing the song of five!" Lisa and Annette sang with the electronic words, voices striving for that mechanical numerical clarity. "Five, five, five, five!" Brian's voice, wordless, equally lucent, chimed in, a braying babble in perfect pitch.

At 5:50 Eliann dumped the pre-washed packaged mixed salad out of its plastic wrapping and into a sleek teak salad bowl. Fluffing it with both her hands, she pulled shreds of red cabbage to the top, and then added, from another plastic package, a handful of alfalfa sprouts to the center. She wanted to set the table early, to allow the bottles of ketchup and creamy green salad dressing to lose their chill. Her hands hesitated inside the dish cabinet, fragile and indecisive as dry oak leaves in autumn wind, between the pale blue Melmac dishes and the heavy speckled-toast ironstone dinner dishes. She felt her heart pound once, hard. She chose the plastic, spared the china.

More things happened. Ron, her husband, got off the 6:10 and into his parked car, heading homeward. Brian threw every one of his toys out of the playpen, and screamed. Neither Lisa nor Annette would pick them up and put them back. Eliann gave orders. Brian threw them all out again and screamed. Eliann broiled the thawed patties, opened a package of frozen corn niblets and threw them into an avocado stainless steel pot, then added margarine and seasoned salt. Lisa and Annette lay the tableware, folded paper napkins, and were trusted to set out the grape jelly glasses, the ones with pictures of Archie and Veronica. Ron arrived home just in time for dinner, as usual, and had frosty autumn kisses for small warm noses. Chill clung to his coat and clean-shaven cheeks and soft pink hands. Lisa reached into his pockets for candy. "After dinner, sugar."

Brian, in the high chair, tried to sing numbers, wordlessly but in pure pitch, spraying crumbled meat all over the floor. Dessert reminded Eliann of grease, and she checked the sunburst corners of wallpaper tiles. Everything was as clean as should be.

More and more things had to happen. Baths and bedtime stories, bunny slippers and Mother Goose pajamas, tuck-ins and dish-washing and putting-away, conversation and television. In the glowing blue light of the bedroom TV, adventures were things that had to happen too. Ron fell asleep first, and Eliann stared into the empty clouds of screen long past the last movie. She fell asleep half-propped up against the pillows, her lower back uncomfortably, familiarly curved and aching. In the first layer of sleep she discovered roses. In the second layer of sleep she discovered the dark, and then, as nothing happened, nothing happened.

Friday afternoon. More rain, silvering the trees and cars and windows and roofs. Eliann, in the entrance hallway, vacuumed the small narrow copy of a Persian rug, its inner medallion composed of two cruciforms, one sand yellow edged in apricot brown, the outer one pale cream, on a wine ground. The emptiness of the inner cruciform pleased her. She vacuumed over and over the inner yellow cross, sucking at the pile until it seemed to glow. She felt as if she were raking sand. For an instant she thought she heard Brian crying, and quickly shut off the machine. Things were strangely still and somewhat grey. It occurred to her she didn't much like Brian, the sound of his voice, or his habits of spilling things and throwing toys around.

Eliann stared into the rug for a long, silent time.

Attar of roses. One large, perfectly-formed, satin-petalled rose, newly opened, dew-spattered, warm as a blush. One rose, trembling at its own existence.

Eliann followed the roar of the vacuum cleaner into the living room. Although she had cleaned there the day before, she gave a quick run-over to the Chinese apricot tree, the flowers and butterflies, and although Brian was still sleeping, she decided to risk the noise of vacuuming the long connecting hallway, with its deep maroon carpeting and the replica of a prayer rug midway down the hall. The prayer rug featured a delicately peaked Ghiordes prayer arch on the inmost medallion, and had a border of geometric motif, leaf-like scrolls within squares, cinnamon, cream and wine. After cleaning the full length of the hallway, and with a strange sense of reluctance, she put away the vacuum cleaner. She passed back through the hallway, burdened by the greyness of the air, the damp ache in her heart. Upon the apex of the prayer arch a small white thread lay, and she knelt to pick it up. No sooner did her knees touch the rug than the essence of roses overpowered her. Shimmering within the arch, the first rose of creation, wet with the dew of paradise, glowed. Her heart beat with the beat of the heart of the rose.

The television camera zoomed backward, and the rose was revealed as one rose in a mass of roses. Eliann saw a thick wall of roses, eight feet high, with an entrance bower of roses arching through the center, roses with satiny petals smooth as a woman's flesh, each thorn two inches long and sharper than daggers. Yet the bower arched high and clear, and a pathway shimmered like pearl-dust, stretching upward along a sward of velvet lawn, a jewel-bright tangle of grasses. Eliann's heart pounded once and exploded with yearning.

She stood up, and carried off in the pinched bird-claw of her right hand the small white thread. Brian would wake up, whimpering, his diaper wet. The girls would come home. Television would sing triumphantly, "Six, six, six, six!" Turkey roll would be heated in the oven, canned cranberry sauce would slide out on a platter bordered with green leaves and orange chrysanthemums. There would be a husband with chill autumn cheeks, scrapy where his beard struggled back, pockets full of candy. A bleak chill, colder than the rainy autumn night, settled damply in her chest.

Late that evening, after the children had eaten their candy and watched one more shred of adventure on TV, after stories and good nights, after coffee and conversation, Ron sat in bed and watched for more among the flickers of excitement, while Eliann, freshly talcum-powdered and dressed in a nightgown of the purest nylon cut to a deep plunging V between her breasts, stood in the hallway outside her bedroom and looked into the tin-bordered Mexican mirror hung at eye level right beside the door. At the mirror she saw, fleetingly, her own face, young enough, pretty enough, gone grey. Through the transparency of her ashen flesh she saw again that pearl-dust path, framed in roses, stretching upward through the velvet grass. At the crest of the hill, way in the distance, was a castle, hard to really see, for it seemed to shift shape, form, color, being now and again cut of hard volcanic black stone, or plated with shimmering gold, now rough-hewn and squat, now thrusting spires like needles into the sky. It was so far and away and changed shape, color, and form, and Eliann gazed up the hill, feeling compelled to walk along the pearl-dust path, through the bower of roses, past green lawns. She heard something chiming like gold through silver air; a harp chord, inverted, shattered against the hard planes of the castle at the top of the hill.

"Eliann!" Eliann followed Ron's call into the bedroom, leaving the mirror behind.

Friday was a love-making night. "Put on your black lace nightie!" His whisper, like sandpaper, was wearing down her listening. She had thought it was a lilac night, but put on the black lace and came back wicked. At the dresser she paused, picked up an atomizer, and hiking up her nightgown and resting one leg on the bed, perfumed her body. She blew a breath of perfume in the direction of the bed, and scrambled into automatic position. Poring over a number of joy books together, they had mutually discovered this variant of the dominant wicked woman, and it worked, often enough, for both of them. Although Eliann ran through the routine expertly, this evening it did not work for her. Ron had told her earlier of a run-in he had had that morning with a subordinate and a dressing-down he had received from a superior that afternoon, so rather than risk making Ron feel insecure, she emitted two passion-torn cries, arching her neck, white and swan-like, upward, and falling across Ron's chest, spent and panting, her hair disheveled and damp with effort. He grunted his appreciation, rolled her off, and reached for a 100g millimeter cigarette. Nostalgia for something she had never known threatened Eliann's field of consciousness, and rather than brood, she slept, bypassing levels of sleep to plunge, as quickly as possible, into nothing, where nothing happened at all.

Lately it seemed as if everything was either flat and grey or led to the scent of roses. Clocks and mirrors, carpets and tiles, the empty smirk of the TV screen, the formal swirling of a flushing toilet, the clear gaze of the wall oven, all were doors. Within the center of things, under peaking arches, in the heart of a tree flowering within a rug, at the center of sunbursts embroidered into pillows was a mist, and in the mist was the scent of roses, and in the scent was a bower and a pathway. One morning, while Brian chewed down the ear of a toy panda, and hurled 27 blocks, one by one, out of the playpen, Eliann passed through the bower and onto the path.

The air smelled of love, new-mown hay and just-fallen rain, cut grasses, decaying forest leaves, freshly baked bread, love. In corners of the island, for she was on an island whose edges shifted within a diamond-sparkling blue sea, mists arose, shaping dreamily into phantasms and dissolving. At the edges of meadows were forests that crept up and then receded, a constantly shifting border of sunlight and deep shadow. Waves crashed against rocks, or lapped calmly upon white beaches. Nothing seemed to hold its shape for long; distances dissolved and re-formed. In the far corner of lawn a triad of girls were playing with a golden ball. Green jeweled snakes mated in clusters among the high grasses. Coming toward Eliann along the pathway were seven figures, golden-haired or capped with copper curls glowing like the rising sun. They were tall and slender, wearing white robes, with huge wings of white feathers folded back against their backs, instead of arms. Out to sea, Eliann saw a single white swan drifting on the waters. Her heart pounded once, with memory. The seven figures drew near, and the tallest and eldest spoke to her in a language that was not English, but which she remembered she had always known and understood, a language round and musical as the spilling of a mountain brook over smooth worn stones. She was welcomed, as a sister, home, by her swan-brothers.

Brian hurled the last block and screamed. Eliann lifted him out of his playpen, sat him on her lap, and loving him no more or less than she would love any child anywhere, taught him how to play pattycake.

On the shifting island, the sun is always in the east, for the island is always furthest to the west. It is always morning, except when it is twilight, and then night. On the shifting island, the coastline makes love to the sea. Brooks follow their own minds, travel one way one day and another way tomorrow. Wells turn into fountains, and fountains into waterfalls, and waterfalls into lakes. Sleek grey seals climb up onto the rocks and become men, and men slip down into the sea and become seals. Sometimes the castle extends a golden drawbridge down to the emerald grass, and all who wish may enter the castle as royalty to revel and feast. Other times there is war, and the castle rises upon a sheer glass mountain, so that only birds or spirits of the air can gain its ground. At such times, when the sky turns blue as midnight and the moon refuses to shine, the spirit of war causes the earth to tremble, and the lords and ladies of the castle gather upon the turrets and watch from their heights, and do not speak or sing. Then they are pale and their eyes are unspeakably sad, and the wind sighs so that any listening to the silence of the castle and the plaint of the air would feel their hearts collapse.

On the shifting island there are many gardens, with all the flowers of forest and meadow arranging themselves in endless patterns of delight. There are lands where only women dwell, and all the women are beautiful, and are young and old as they please.

Here is music with harp and flute and drum and bell, and here is dancing and singing in chains and rings. Eliann wandered along island pathways, dwelt in the gardens, explored the dark forests, stood at the shores of the endless sea. She sheltered for a while in the land of women and learned all the arts invented by women. She stood in time of war at the base of the glass mountain and saw the silent lords and ladies, and heard the battle of air elements, and was afraid. Evenings she reveled in the great halls of the castle, laughed at the wisdom of the jester, and was moved beyond words by the songs of the poets.

On the shifting island Eliann made love to seal-men upon the rocks at the edge of grey and stormy waters in soft and misty air, and learned all the secrets of the world from the stories of her swan-brothers, who had flown everywhere, seen everything, and knew the language of the birds.

Lisa had German measles, and then so did Annette, but Brian slept in his own room and was lucky and didn't get sick. Eliann nursed the two girls with as much love as she would feel for any child born on earth to suffer and die. Christmas came. Ron and Eliann had a fight about the tree, again. Eliann, as usual, was afraid that a real tree would catch fire and burn down the house, and Ron insisted that an artificial tree was not in the spirit of Christmas. Again they had a real tree, because Eliann again realized that her fears were unfounded, and that she was just being a big paranoid baby. Something turned flat and grey as she realized that it didn't much matter if the house and all the furniture and children burned to the ground.

Christmas eve they spread a sheet on the rug, bunching it up to look like a snowy landscape, and laid out the crèche, very expensive and hand carved in either Germany or Poland, Eliann could never remember and Ron never knew. There were many toys: dolls, stuffed animals, child-sized kitchens, miniature brooms and carpet-sweepers and irons, tiny trucks and cars and a fire engine big enough to sit on and ride about. There were packages and packages of clothes: new bunny slippers in the new right sizes, Mother Goose pajamas, mittens and scarves and socks and tiny fur muffs that also were pocketbooks. Toys and toys and toys and things.

Eliann got the new tapestry needlepoint kit she had long wanted, with the hunting scene and the horses. Annette dislocated her shoulder in nursery playgroup on the slide into the sandbox. Ron and Eliann found a new picture in one of the joy books, showing something very complicated and holy called the cradle of the lotus, which meant they both had to sit conjoined facing each other and Eliann was supposed to be in control while Ron thought about other things so that their spirits could unite. After two weeks of uniting spirits Ron brought home from his favorite specialty lingerie store in the city a black lace cut-out bra and garters with red ribbons.

When Eliann completed the tapestry she hung it where she could see it while sitting on a straight-backed chair, and after that there were horses and hunting on the shifting island.

Ron did not get a long-coveted promotion, but his closest friend on the job did, and Ron brought home rubber novelties and magazines from an adult book store, and convinced Eliann that using such "marital aids" was perfectly natural and desirable, based on page 83 of one manual and page 127 of another.

Eliann no longer watched the TV yoga show, but went straight to the mirror or the clock or the rug and disappeared into the mists and the roses until Brian or the oven timer or the ringing telephone needed her.

One night Ron wanted to spank Eliann because she wore black lace and was wicked, and they had a big fight, and the next night he brought home another tapestry needlepoint kit, showing the unicorn and the maiden, so that Eliann was frightened and wept.

On the shifting island the unicorn walks free and young girls play with golden balls, and snakes of green and jeweled splendor copulate at the heels of dancers, and no one offends the other. After the wars, heroes are borne through the air to the castle upon the glass mountain, and are given honey-wine to drink in golden cups. Poets tell songs of heroes and lovers and animals who change their shapes, of ravens who become fish, of fish who become panthers, of panthers who become doves, of doves who become wolves, of wolves who become trees, of trees chained to the earth by mistletoe. Harp strings are made of gold as bright as the blonde hair of girls from the land where only women dwell.

The Queen whose name is never said asked that Eliann have private audience with her. Eliann's hair was dressed with jewels and flowers, and her feet were washed and perfumed. The Queen wore a robe golden as the sun, entwined all over with green vines, which writhed and tangled upon her belly and breasts, transforming into fruit and flower and fishes and birds. Upon her hair she wore a crown silver as the moon.

"You walk away from us, through the rose bower, and disappear."

"Yes." Brian rattled the bars of his crib. He wanted to run around on the floor, to find dust in the corners to eat, to overturn lamps and lick electrical sockets and piss on the rug.

"Wherever you look, you find us again."

"Yes." The yellow bus stood in front of the house, and the driver waited, with that surly look on his face, for Eliann to open the door and let Lisa come home.

"You find gateways in all you possess, and despise what you possess. You come to us, and then you pass through the impenetrable wall of roses and disappear."

"Yes." Coffee was growing cold in a pale blue Melmac cup.

"Time cannot always serve you. Soon the gateways will harden. One day you will walk away from us once too many a time, through the rose bower, and you will turn to ash upon the threshold, burned by time."

"Yes." Dust was collecting in all the corners.

"You will stare at the surfaces of things and find them only surfaces, frigid and implacable. You will be left with only your possessions, your world, and your life. You will live, grow old and ill, suffer, and die. Your last few months of life will find you a body devouring itself, lying in a hospital bed, with tubes in your nose, your throat, and your urethra, while they watch your energy by its feeble flickering in a system of colored lights above your bed. You will smell bad and feel great pain. Nothing will yield to your stare."

"Yes." A chain of automobile lights colored the highway night.

"Eliann, the time is coming when you will have to make a choice. You cannot live here and there. Go tend your house and children and husband. The next time you see the rose and come home to the island will be the last opening of the gates. You must come in forever, or never come in at all."

"Yes." The telephone rang. Eliann's neighbor was crying her usual story into the phone. It seemed her husband was working late again, and had called to say he might not come home at all. He had recently fired a used-up secretary and hired a new one.

The TV sang, crisp as a new dollar bill. "Seven, seven, seven, seven!" Annette and Lisa and Brian sang along, their voices ringing like a pocket full of change.

Eliann stood at the kitchen door, watching evening clouds scudding westward into the tattered gilt of sunset. A last frenzy of birdcall stirred the saplings planted along the borders of the yard. Fat green buds had newly opened, and crocus huddled in a white and saffron mass by the fence. The barbecue grill was cold and rusted. Eliann thought that she was tired of spring. She hummed a little tune, a descending arpeggio once heard on a harp, that resolved and then flared up again.

Eliann remembered the advice in magazines and manuals, remembered that desserts were tokens of love, remembered instant whipped cream and black lace cut-out bras, morning exercises and emptying the mind with the master on TV. She did not love her husband, that she knew. Nor did she love her children, bland and smooth and sweet as whipped cream. Nor her neighbor nor her needlepoint. There was nothing in the whole world, dry and angry as hell, that she loved. There was nothing to hold her here, that she knew, as sure as she knew the scent of roses and the nostalgia for something she had never known.

In the kitchen Eliann picked up a shred of song where she had left it, something she had heard many times on the radio. She poured a cup of coffee and stared at the golden point of the clock, for it was six o'clock for a long time. The golden point wavered, a thin liquid mirror about to part, to reveal something ancient and submarine. The scent of roses, the one rose, the bower, the path. The Queen whose name is never said stood on the threshold, her breasts bare, her welcoming arms upraised, golden snakes clutched in her hands, while a snake curled around her waist like a girdle. A melody golden as the hair of young women hovered around the strings of a harp, lingered in the dark hollows of a flute.

Eliann, who loved neither house nor child nor husband nor friend, stood with her feet upon the grim surfaces of things, in a world in which spring always would be grey and pale, a world flat and dour, without reason or beauty or hope. She knew the Queen whose name is never said as she knew herself, knew her as a mother. She saw the love and welcome in her eyes. And turned away into the kitchen, toward the freezer, to pull out two packages of frozen Chinese food for dinner. In the bleak grey kitchen, without love or reason or beauty or hope, Eliann waited for the rest of the world to need what she knew about what she had lost.

www.ingramcontent.com/pod-product-compliance
Lightning Source LLC
Chambersburg PA
CBHW070446170726
48291CB00005B/1626

* 9 7 8 1 9 4 9 0 9 3 1 1 7 *